# LEATHER ROGUES

# LEATHER ROGUES

A SHORT STORY ANTHOLOGY BY

## BILL LEE

GLB Publishers, San Francisco          First Edition

Published in the United States by
GLB Publishers
P.O. Box 78212, San Francisco, CA 94107 USA

Number 2 of ROGUES Series

Cover Design by Timothy Lewis and W.L. Warner

ISBN 1-879194-01-5

First printing, February, 1991
Reprinted 1992
10  9  8  7  6  5  4  3  2

# FOREWORD BY THE AUTHOR

The stories included here are explicit gay male action, and make no pretense at teaching or endorsing any particular activity. It is recognized that many of the scenes include activities that are risky in the age of AIDS with unfamiliar partners. The author believes that fiction can be used as a substitute for risk-taking; if these pages become sticky, they may have succeeded in preventing transmission of the AIDS virus.

Names, characters, places, and incidents are either the products of the author's imagination or are used fictitiously, and any resemblance to actual persons, living or dead, events, or locales is entirely coincidental.

To all the slaves who taught me,
in their way, to be myself, and
especially to John.

# TABLE OF CONTENTS

# FIRST RITES

"THE NAIL", the sign read in flickering blue neon above the stark, black facade of the West Side bar, a very different appearance than most bars he knew, but he knew this one was different. He had been told this was a leather bar, and even though his palms were sweaty, he was determined to explore, to expose himself to this world which seemed to hold tremendous allure side by side with satanic threat. He hoped he was dressed at least suitably, glancing down at his levis and suede jacket.

A pale sliver of light shone under the door and the thud of rock music punctuated the air as he approached. After only a moment's hesitation, Tom pushed open the door and strode to the bar directly inside. He resolved not even to look around until he had beer in hand and could take his time. A paunchy bartender in a leather vest handed him a cold one. The liquid had a welcome snap to his tongue, but the mirror behind the bar was smoky; Tom turned and leaned back against the polished wood to survey the room.

Immediately he became aware of a heady aroma, the pervasive and excitingly masculine fragrance of leather wafting to his alerted nostrils. The odor was almost an aphrodisiac - he felt his cock stir in his levis. He inhaled deeply several times, wallowing in the sensuality of the masculine images forming in his awakening brain.

He also became aware of several pairs of eyes studying him with interest. Perhaps it was his clothes, he thought. Most of the guys were dressed in black leather jackets, pants, caps, and engineer boots. The leather gleamed dully in the dim light, set off by steel belt buckles, eagles on the caps, and chains or rings hanging from the epaulets of their jackets. Some wore leather chaps which covered the legs, leaving the packed crotches and buttocks open

1

to reveal faded levis beneath.

Tom was acutely aware that his jacket was suede, not shiny black; that his low boots had zippers in them; that he really didn't understand the scene but he knew he wanted to. At that moment he was startled by a heavy hand descending on his shoulder.

"New here, aren't you?" inquired a deep but not unfriendly voice. Tom turned to meet twinkling blue eyes under thick, dark brows set in a rugged face outlined by a clipped beard. Their eyes surveyed each other openly.

"Yes, I am," he responded directly, " - but I think I belong here." He was surprised to hear himself say it.

The bearded smile broadened. He introduced himself as "Jack" and mentioned that he sometimes acted as interference if the wrong people started to come into the bar.

"Why did you let me in?" Tom inquired. Jack looked him up and down for a moment. His voice was low and gruff.

"You're OK. You're a man. You'll learn," and then he sauntered away.

There wasn't much time to ponder this mysterious pronouncement. At that moment two men entered the bar together and Tom's attention was immediately captured.

The taller of the two was broad shouldered and narrow hipped. He wore leather pants, jacket, and cap, and under the jacket a leather shirt closed with leather thongs. Wiry black hair curled from the open neck. His eyes were deep-set and blue, contrasting sharply with his black hair worn low on his neck. He wore heavy engineer boots.

Several inches shorter and thirty pounds lighter, the smaller man had light brown hair, brown eyes, and a small mustache which accentuated his finer features. He wore chaps over worn levis which were torn over one ass cheek; those firm buns and the glimpse of pale skin were enough to start Tom's cock growing.

He sensed that they were discussing him as they stood at the bar gulping beer. Finally they both turned to look directly at him. Tom returned their interest with a hesitant smile.

They walked over to him and took swigs of beer before speaking. The taller man held Tom's gaze; he was apparently the leader - or should he be called a master? Tom wondered.

"My name's Steve. What's yours?"

"It's Tom." He glanced at the smaller man standing slightly to Steve's rear.

"This is my boy, Dorn," Steve answered the unspoken question and grasped Tom's hand in a heavy fist. "Are you slumming or do you like it here?" His gaze swept over the suede jacket and levis but settled for a moment on the impressive bulge in the groin. The abrupt frankness of the question startled Tom. He flushed, explaining that it was his first time in the bar. Both men studied him silently for a moment.

"What are you into?" Steve finally asked.

Tom hesitated before answering. "To tell the truth, I'm not sure."

Again both men contemplated him silently for a moment. Still Dorn had not uttered a word. Tom guessed that this was part of his role, to remain in Steve's background. As if to prove him wrong, Dorn finally spoke in a surprisingly husky voice. "We're ready to help you make up your mind, if you're interested."

Tom's cock gave a lurch. "You mean a three-way?"

Steve nodded. "Something like that. Dorn is my slave. I think I know how it will work out, but you must decide for yourself. Whatdya say?"

The handsome virility and the direct approach of the Master and slave stirred his curiosity but mostly aroused his sexual lust. On top of it all, that sensuous aroma of leather...

"I say yeah."

Both men grinned. "Are you driving?" Steve asked and Tom nodded. "We're on the bikes. You can follow us to our place in the village."

It was a short trip. Tom waited at the entrance while Steve and Dorn parked their motorcycles in the underground garage. Then they climbed to the third floor apartment. It was plainly furnished with low comfortable furniture and a minimum of wall decoration. Dorn brought three beers from the refrigerator and after a few gulps they moved into the bedroom.

This room was almost as large as the living room and contained a king sized bed covered with black leather and pillows encased in black leather as well. Two dim red bulbs in recesses furnished the only illumination. At both ends of the room was a large closet.

Both Steve and Dorn seemed to change upon entering the room. Steve's eyes took on a stern light and Dorn waited behind him with head bowed. Steve stood for a moment with his arms folded, staring at Tom, and then in a commanding voice said to Dorn, "Put on your harness."

Dorn meekly turned to the closet. When he opened the doors wide, Tom was startled to see a vast assortment of leather straps, belts, harnesses, whips, and dildoes hung neatly in readiness for use; from the top of the door immediately inside, several hooks could be seen.

Dorn quickly stripped off his clothes, revealing a neat, trim body with a scattering of light brown hair on his chest and legs, becoming a thick nest at his groin. His circumcised cock was on its way to full erection. His nipples were unusually large and protruded sharply, and Tom wondered if they had been enlarged by his Master in their private play. As the slave bent over to remove his socks, that round, creamy ass that had set Tom's cock astir in the bar came up for inspection. Tom unconsciously fingered his lengthening cock, his eyes fixed on the dark valley and its promise of pleasure.

Without changing expression, Steve winked at Tom, knowing what was taking place in his head.

Dorn stood up, the leather harness in place. The straps were wide and interrupted at regular spaces by grommets. There were rings on both shoulders and the belt was wide. Below the belt was a flat piece of leather extending to the crotch; in this piece was a hole through which Dorn was somewhat painfully stuffing his cock and balls so they stood out proudly from that compact body. Narrow straps attached the frontispiece around the back and between the legs to the belt at the sides, leaving the ass completely exposed. Next Dorn picked up a broad leather collar and handed it meekly to his Master.

Steve pulled Dorn around roughly and fastened the collar around the neck of his slave, who then stood with bowed head awaiting the next command. Both men were completely ignoring Tom; this was a ritual between Master and slave only, but Tom was becoming more turned on by the minute. Steve was still fully dressed in his shiny black leather.

"On your knees," he barked, and Dorn immediately complied, beginning to nuzzle Steve's boots. "Clean them up!" was the next command, and Dorn began to lap the boots free of road dirt accumulated during their motorcycle ride through Manhattan. The leather was soon damp and shiny as Dorn eagerly cleaned the boots with his tongue, his ass bobbing around and increasing Tom's fever.

"Now work your way up," Steve snarled, and Dorn continued his ministrations up the leather pants, first one leg and then the other. By this time a huge bulge was evident at Steve's crotch, and Dorn started to nibble and lick the leather covering this bulge as he reached the crotch.

"I didn't tell you you could have that!" Steve growled, and Dorn immediately left that enticing mound to continue his cleaning duties. He moved to Steve's ass, licking the leather clean and spending more time in the crack along the leather seam. Steve spread his legs to allow this service.

Dorn then proceeded up the opening of the leather shirt, inserting his tongue through the gap to lap the curly black chest hair of his Master. When he encountered a leather thong, he bit and sucked it briefly. Finally he was at the neck, and he ran his tongue around the neckline and under the chin line, into the ears of his Master but carefully avoiding the mouth.

Steve's expression remained blank. He stood stock-still with his hands arrogantly placed on his hips, confident of his authority over his slave.

When he was satisfied, he commanded, "Take off the clothes, starting with the boots." Dorn hastened to comply. Steve lifted one foot and Dorn slowly removed the boot; he then stripped off the sock and held it tightly to his nose for a moment to savor his Master's foot odor. Then holding the foot gently, he began to tongue it eagerly, licking the instep, the sole, the heel, and carefully between each toe. Steve grunted when he decided it was enough, and Dorn then moved to the other foot to minister to it in the same way.

"Now the jacket," Steve barked, and Dorn, still on his knees, raised his head to unzip the sleeves with his teeth. He rose to stand behind Steve and slowly lifted the jacket from his Master's shoulders. For a moment he buried his face in the jacket, breathing in his Master's odor and the leather aroma, and then placed the jacket on the bed.

Returning to Steve, he eagerly unfastened the shirt thongs with his teeth and spread the shirt with his hands

6

while licking his Master's chest as he went. More and more of the massive chest was exposed, and finally the small, firm nipples came into view. Dorn spent several minutes on each nub, tonguing them until they stood out sharply and then tenderly biting and sucking. Steve merely closed his eyes, but it was apparent to Tom that the sensation was exquisitely pleasurable. Tom unconsciously touched his own nipples through his shirt, vicariously enjoying the treatment.

Finally Dorn began to roll the shirt up that broad chest. It fit snugly, and it was with some difficulty that he managed to raise it to the sweaty armpits. He eagerly pressed his tongue and nose into those damp recesses and began to lick the hair as he inhaled deeply. He obviously enjoyed the odor of healthy mansweat and leather in this hairy spot. Then Steve lifted his arms and Dorn stripped the shirt above the shoulders. The Master dropped his head and arms and Dorn removed the shirt, careful not to disturb the cap still firmly placed on Steve's head. Without being told, he replaced the jacket on his Master and stood meekly, waiting for the next command.

"The belt," Steve said flatly. Immediately Dorn pulled the heavy leather through its keeper and, still with his teeth, pulled it back to free the buckle. Then he pulled the thick leather out and the belt hung loose in front. He looked up at his Master, and Steve nodded briefly. The slave's teeth fastened over the leather waist band and pulled the snap open at the top of the fly. He grasped the zipper tab between his teeth and slowly pulled it down. As the pants parted, more and more of that wiry black body hair was revealed and then the root of the cock was visible. Dorn lapped and licked the black bush, starting at the navel, which received extra attention. He worked his way down to the crotch and finally placed his mouth over the thick stem which was the only part available. He buried his nose in the leather crotch, inhaling deeply and tonguing the cock root.

Then, by grasping the outside seams of the trouser legs, he very slowly inched the leather pants down, revealing more and more of his Master's massive prick. He ran his tongue and lips up and down the shaft as it was exposed. Finally the mammoth tool sprang free of the leather, standing out proudly in all its ten-inch glory. It was heavy and thick, throbbing in its excitement, the exposed head shiny and damp with pre-cum fluid.

Dorn groaned with pleasure but knew he was not yet allowed to service that cock as deserved. Instead he began to lap the huge balls now exposed in their hairy sack.

"Be good to those balls," Steve growled. "That's where you next load is coming from." Dorn continued to suck and lick the balls, wetting the coarse black hair and sucking each sphere in turn into his mouth, then releasing it.

"You may take one trip down the prick," Steve grunted. Dorn hastened to transfer his attention to the broad head of the jutting meat. He licked off the fluid collecting at the tip and ran his tongue around the ridge. The prick throbbed and jerked although Steve's stern expression did not change. Dorn took the pulsing head in his mouth and slowly advanced down the thick stalk, moving his tongue constantly along the underside.

Tom watched as inch after inch disappeared into Dorn's mouth. The slave was obviously an expert because soon it was impaled in his throat. He took a breath and then forced it all the way down and held it there without gagging. Steve's eyes were again closed, but it was not possible for him to maintain his stolid expression any longer. The sensation of his cock all the way down that hot, wet throat, with Dorn's tongue still teasing the underside, brought a grimace to his face that revealed his ecstasy. But he stood perfectly still, his mouth working, until Dorn was forced to move back up the shaft to take a breath. Then he held the cockhead in his mouth until Steve stepped back a pace.

Tom could stand it no longer. He was inflamed with the sight of this prince of a man being serviced by the handsome boy, and he fumbled at his own fly. He had to grasp his hot cock or at least release it from its confinement.

Steve noticed Tom's actions and barked, "Stop!" Tom looked at him in confusion. More gently Steve said, "My boy will take care of you."

Dorn turned to Tom with a smile and murmured, "Yes, Sir." He moved on his knees to Tom's feet and asked, "What do you wish, Sir?" Steve smiled encouragingly at Tom and gripped his own cock in his hairy fist.

So this is what they meant by a three-way, Tom thought as he tried to adjust his whirling brain to the situation. He had several choices - he could tear off his clothes and join this manly pair in whatever happened; he could certainly be happy with that massive cock in his mouth; he hoped to fuck the handsome boy at his feet, and he was sorely tempted to do just that as soon as possible. The aroma of leather and male sweat in the room was intoxicating, and he felt sure that whatever these guys wanted to do would be extremely satisfying for him. All he had to do was drop his pants.

But the boy with the slave collar and harness was looking up at him expectantly, awaiting orders. Steve was grinning at him while slowly stroking that huge dick, like a gladiator in his leather jacket with the chain over his left shoulder. Obviously just stripping would not be in harmony with the scene he was privileged to participate in, and it appeared that Steve had pegged Tom as a master, or at least a potential one. It was a time for decision, Tom realized dimly - but then he realized clearly that there was only one answer, one reaction appropriate for him at that moment.

9

"Take off my boots," he ordered sternly. Dorn smiled fleetingly and began to remove the boots. Steve's grin widened but he stood still, stroking his prick with both hands but not enough to bring on climax.

The boots and socks removed, Dorn began to wash Tom's feet with his tongue. Tom had never experienced this before and it sent chills up his spine. Dorn held one foot in his hand and licked first the top, then the sides, and finally slurped across the sole of the foot. This set Tom's head reeling, but then Dorn set to washing his toes one by one with the moist, darting tongue. Whenever his tongue dipped between his toes, Tom shivered with joy. His face was contorted in his effort to remain standing patiently under this pressure.

Then Dorn moved to the other foot and repeated the process. Again Tom almost shouted with pleasure but remained composed this time. The boy looked up at Tom, his surrogate master, and asked, "How may I serve you now, Sir?"

"My shirt," Tom answered hoarsely. Dorn immediately unbuttoned the sleeves at the wrist and pulled the shirt out of the top of the levis. He unbuttoned it, exposing Tom's navel. His tongue darted into that little valley and rimmed it enticingly, wetting the hairs that surrounded it. Tom's belly lurched with excitement.

Dorn continued to work his way up, licking the broad chest with its curly, black hairs, spreading his attention out over the rib cage and sending Tom's head spinning with the exquisite pleasure of his service. As the chest was gradually revealed, Dorn's pleasure was apparent from the humming sounds in this throat - and all with the permission of his Master!

He fastened his mouth to Tom's nipple and began to lick and suck and tease it. Tom writhed under his treatment and his cock gave a lurch in his levis. Again Tom wished he could release his cock, but that was not part of the role he had decided upon. He stood resolutely with his hands on his hips while Dorn serviced his other nipple. By this time, Tom was gritting his teeth with the effort to remain still.

Dorn stood upright and eased the shirt off Tom's broad shoulders. While behind him, he licked his way down the midline of his back and then along the outlines of the back muscles so well defined, then around the lower edge of the rib cage, and down to the waist where the levis blocked further travel. Tom's head was thrown back in joy. Dorn ended his trip by burying his nose in Tom's armpits and licking the damp skin and hair there until Tom nearly collapsed from the exquisite sensation. He was beginning to realize the extension of limits of erotic enjoyment that these guys understood.

Dorn again knelt at his feet awaiting further instructions. Tom's fly was still open from his aborted plan to take out his cock by himself. The slave's eyes followed the huge bulge that the throbbing hard-on made in his levis. He licked his lips and looked up at Tom pleadingly.

Tom stepped forward, mashing his stiff covered prick against Dorn's face. The boy licked at the bulge until the levis were wet, and he groaned in anticipation of the enormity inside. Tom shoved the brown head roughly into his crotch with both hands, grinding the covered cock and balls against the straining face. Dorn looked up happily at this treatment and then closed his eyes to savor the moment.

When Tom released him, Dorn was attracted by the black pubic hair protruding from the gaping fly. He started licking those hairs one by one, his tongue also lapping the belly skin. He moved up and down the open fly, lapping skin and hair until Tom could stand it no longer.

Forsaking his role, Tom ripped open his levis and yanked them part of the way to his knees. His massive cock sprang out at full attention, demanding release. When Dorn saw the beautiful cock bobbing in his face, his mouth formed an ◯ and he began to pant with desire.

Steve also nodded appreciatively. He and Tom could have been twins as far as cock was concerned - both about ten inches long, both circumcised, both set in a bush of curly black hair, and both ready for action!

Now that his cock was free, Tom felt better. He gripped it with both hands and began to stroke it slowly, tilted up to bring his hairy balls in Dorn's face. "Suck my balls, slave!" he commanded, and Dorn was only too happy to comply. His moist tongue reached out and cradled each one, licking gently and sucking the hairs into his mouth. He also ran his tongue down behind the balls between the spread legs toward the asshole. Then he returned to the heavy orbs as Tom continued to milk his cock slowly.

The working tongue of the serving boy set Tom's senses reeling, and copious pre-cum dripped from the twitching prick. Steve moved to Tom's side to share his scene with him. It seemed that Tom was now taking responsibility for the Master's role.

He lowered his rod so it pointed directly at Dorn's mouth, but he still held it firmly. The broad head was only inches away from that haven where it would soon be lodged. Dorn hesitantly licked up the pre-cum dripping from the pulsing cockhead. He was not sure he had permission. Tom did not object, but stiffened as the moist tonguetip touched. Then abruptly, holding his cock just behind the head, he pushed the slave's head down, filling his mouth with the mushroom knob.

Dorn sucked the spongy meat greedily, licking all around it and nibbling the loose skin of the frenulum and then applying more tongue lashing. Tom couldn't take much of that so he dropped his hands, allowing the entire cock to hang free. Dorn looked up expectantly.

12

"Suck it!" Tom gritted.

"Oh, yes, Sir!" Dorn murmured. He plunged as far down the long shaft as he could in one gulp. He twisted his head around the huge tool, moving his tongue furiously and causing Tom's knees to buckle. Then the cocksucker tried to force the throbbing head all the way down his throat, but the dickhead was larger than Steve's and it was more difficult. Finally, by tilting his head back, he accomplished it, a feat never achieved before. The loaded balls rested on Dorn's chin, the black pubic hair mixing with Dorn's lighter mustache. The boy could not hold it for long, though, and he moved back, twirling his tongue and twisting his head while Tom groaned in joy.

Steve placed a burly arm around Tom's shoulders to steady him. That leather-clad arm against Tom's skin and the hairy chest against his side, that rugged face only inches away, that hot mouth on his prick, all combined to fill the moment with fulfilled fantasy for Tom. Dorn continued his expert sucking and Steve tightened his grip on Tom's shoulder.

Tom put one arm around Steve and began massaging one nipple as Dorn picked up his pace. Saliva was dripping from the huge cock and Dorn used it to moisten and caress the heavy balls as he sucked avidly.

Tom had almost climaxed with Dorn's first dive down his rampant rod. He had held back then, but Dorn's avid sucking, his sweet strokes on his churning balls, and Steve's pressure on his shoulders combined to reduce his control. He felt early spasms in his balls, telling him the time was near. Steve turned from watching his lover sucking cock and saw the imminence of Tom's surge. Their eyes met in deep man-to-man gaze. As the crescendo built inside Tom, their faces moved nearer and their lips finally met in a profound tongue-lashing, soul-searching, groaning kiss just as Tom's balls exploded and he gushed geysers of steamy cum into Dorn's hungry throat.

Spurt after spurt bathed Dorn's gulping craw as he sucked on the delicious nectar. Tom's entire body was afire, lurching repeatedly against Steve who held him in an iron grasp, shoving his tongue down Tom's throat as far as it would go. Tom sucked in the thick tongue as greedily as Dorn sucked his prick dry. At length, Tom sagged weakly and Steve eased him down to lie quivering on the leather-covered bed.

Tom's eyes closed and he gasped long, deep breaths through his open mouth. The leather felt rough and solid under his back, and a few drops of oozing cum dribbled down to puddle on the leather. Dorn licked it up, still hungry for the potent cream.

When Tom's breathing was more regular and his pulse had slowed somewhat, Dorn placed one of the leather-covered pillows under his head. Steve lay down beside him on his stomach, one arm thrown over Tom's chest. Immediately Dorn buried his face between those solid ass cheeks of his Master, first licking around the edges and gradually zeroing in on that entrance that he loved so much. As Tom watched, the slave stiffened his tongue and inserted it into the asshole deeply; he then moved it in circles, in and out, causing Steve to grunt and moan appreciatively.

Tom's cock started to rise again as he watched the devoted service close at hand. Steve moved a leather pillow under his own hips to elevate them, trapping his cock between the pillow and his belly, and allowing Dorn to rim his asshole more effectively. Steve's hip movements stroked the huge, stiff cock against the pillow, and soon it was wet with pre-cum juices. Dorn's face was concealed by the writhing asscheeks. Tom found himself jerking his stiffened cock as he watched the slave serving his Master.

Abruptly Steve stood up, moved the pillow aside, and pushed Dorn down on the bed on his back next to Tom.

He straddled Dorn's face and pushed his big balls into Dorn's mouth. The slave sucked the hot orbs greedily until Steve pulled away and moved up to place his asshole squarely over Dorn's mouth.

"Clean out that shit-chute!" he barked, and Dorn increased his efforts with his tongue. Steve's cock rested on Dorn's forehead, just inches from Tom's face. Tom could see every vein and fine hair on that beautiful organ, the skin moving smoothly as Steve moved his ass on Dorn's face.

Tom could not resist grasping that thick cock. His fist could not reach all the way around it. It was hot and throbbing, the skin loose and smooth. Tom moved his fist up and down a few times, milking that magnificent prick, and then pushed the cock down hard on Dorn's face, moving it around his forehead, in his hair, and over the ears. Dorn moaned, his voice muffled by his Master's ass. The slave's cock and balls stood up sharply, throbbing in their leather harness. Steve's head was thrown back in ecstasy. He was close to cumming, but wanted to postpone it a while.

Again he pulled away before he reached his peak. He roughly lifted Dorn by his harness and hauled him to the leather closet., motioning for Tom to join them there. He fastened chains from the hooks above the door to Dorn's shoulder straps, adjusting the length to suit his plans. He then bent Dorn down so the weight of his upper body was supported by the chains with his ass up and exposed. He selected a medium-sized leather dildo from the assortment in the closet, smeared lubricant on it, and slowly but firmly inserted it into Dorn's ass.

Dorn groaned with the sudden invasion. This was his Master's wish and he had no choice but to accept it.

Steve worked the dildo in and out of that compact ass, his own cock riding back and forth over the same asscheeks. Tom was now openly jerking his cock in envy of the dildo.

Steve motioned for Tom to replace the dildo with his cock. Tom was certainly ready for that. The Master pulled out the long leather dildo and smeared some grease on Tom's stiff prick, giving it a few rough jerks for his own pleasure. This turned Tom on even more. Then Steve held the slippery cockhead against his slave's closed asshole and Tom buried his dick to the hilt in one slamming thrust.

That hot, gripping ass engulfing his cock, his balls pressed tightly against those firm asscheeks, and the moaning willingness of the leather-harnessed ass slave was almost enough to push Tom over the edge immediately. He stopped moving to allow his excitement to subside, but Dorn began massaging his embedded cock with his ass muscles, bringing a moan to Tom's lips. That silken tunnel around his overheated prick was exquisitely tantalizing.

Satisfied with the connection, Steve moved in front of Dorn and shoved his cock roughly into the boy's mouth. Dorn was now impaled on both ends with almost identical hot, throbbing pricks. Tom pulled almost all the way out, riding over Dorn's prostate, and then shoved it in all the way. Dorn pushed back, demanding all Tom could give him. His own smaller cock throbbed and jerked with every movement. He wrapped his arms around his Master's brawny, hairy legs and sucked that beautiful cock deep into his throat.

Steve held Dorn's head firmly with both hands, fucking his face as he knew Dorn liked it. Tom grasped the leather harness and pulled the slave toward him as he lunged in and out with increasing speed. The sight of the leather Master face-fucking his slave and his own soaring thrill from burying his cock into the same handsome slave was too much for Tom to bear for long.

As he watched Steve's face he could see his climax

16

arriving inevitably - the mouth became distorted and the handsome head was thrown back in gasping joy. Suddenly his head snapped forward and he stared directly into Tom's eyes. "Now!" he shouted.

Both cocks gushed their loads into the struggling boy at the same time, flooding his mouth and ass with spurts of hot jism. Both men continued to piston in and out, their balls pulled up and contracting, giving up their delicious fluid. Still holding Dorn's head, Steve fucked the gasping face until he finally stopped spurting, and Tom, growing weak in the knees, tapered off in that gorgeous ass. Dorn was gurgling with happiness, filled with the man-cream he loved so much. Finally he was released to swing alone on the chains.

Dorn was left hanging both literally and sexually. His legs were trembling from the experience and his cock was jerking painfully, needing release. Without thinking he grabbed it and began to jerk it, but Steve roused himself and slapped Dorn's hand away. He had not given Dorn permission to touch his cock.

Steve unfastened the chains on Dorn's shoulders and pushed him down on his back on the bed. From the corners of the bed, already in position, he brought manacles which he fastened to both wrists and ankles.

The handsome boy, his trim body stretched out on the black leather, tied by leather straps and completely at the mercy of his Master, was a vision to be stamped in Tom's memory. The boy's seven-inch cock was throbbing and purple from frustration. Tom's cock began to rise again.

Steve went to the closet and returned with a cat-o'-nine-tails, a whip with a short leather handle dotted with steel studs, and many leather thongs approximately three feet long. Tom could see that Steve's cock was also rising again.

Steve introduced the whip by drawing it slowly up Dorn's legs, each thong caressing its separate course. A couple of the thongs nudged the swollen balls as the whip was drawn up over groin, belly, and chest. Dorn sighed, "Oh, yes, Master," and then was silent. Tom again had his cock in his fist, as did Steve.

Suddenly Steve brought the whip down sharply over Dorn's legs, leaving red streaks where each thong had slashed. The boy twitched but remained silent. Steve then expertly snapped the whip to touch and sting the boy's nipples, each time met by a lurch of the body laid out before him. Dorn's face wore a rapt smile.

The Master returned his attention to the legs, moving up toward the groin with each stroke. As the thongs lashed his balls, Dorn moaned again, still smiling. His cock was even larger now, the head swelling as if it might burst. Tom felt the same way. Steve continued to jerk his own cock with one hand while manipulating the whip with the other. This time he brought it down directly on the cock and balls, and Dorn screamed.

Tom's prick strained in his hand, close again to orgasm. Steve was breathing hard also, but not from physical exertion. He brought the whip down again and again with increasing ferocity on the boy's cock and balls, and suddenly cum shot high in the air from the bruised prick as the slave screamed again. The cock jerked wildly as spurt after spurt fell back on his belly, his chest, and some even striking his face from the violence of his orgasm.

Steve dropped the whip and knelt on the bed, jerking his own load into Dorn's face as the slave continued to jet his load. Tom also started spurting in Dorn's face, his cum mixing with Steve's, cream spraying and dribbling into the boy's eyes, his hair, and some into his gaping mouth. Two hairy fists jerked two magnificent pricks, spurting gobs of manjuice onto the handsome face.

As soon as their crises subsided, Steve bent and gathered some of the mixed cum in his mouth. He kissed his slave-lover deeply, sharing the cream with the boy who had missed swallowing the final loads. Then Dorn relaxed with a sigh. "Thank you, Sir," he murmured.

Steve released the bonds and the three men stretched out of the bed entwined, their eyes closed in contentment. Sleep came to Tom in a rush; it was the first night in many years that he slept in total sexual satisfaction.

* * *

It must have been about two hours later that the mists began to clear. Slowly he opened his eyes to the dim red light of the leather room. He started to move and could not. Suddenly he jerked to full wakefulness - his wrists and ankles were shackled securely; he was tied spread-eagled on the leather-covered bed, completely naked and unable to move!

Craning his neck, he saw two shrouded figures - two men with black leather hoods covering their faces with openings only for their eyes and mouths. They stood silently by the bed, looking down at him like executioners or avengers, watching his reactions, waiting for the full impact of his predicament to penetrate his sleep-fogged brain.

The taller figure wore a leather loin-piece - a wide leather strap over his hairy belly, held in place by narrow straps in the back, all attached to a wide leather belt with studs. Snapped to the front piece was a softer leather pouch enclosing his cock and balls. His broad chest with its matted black hair, the thick bulging calves and thighs covered with black fur, and the black leather-masked head sent chills of apprehension through Tom's straining body.

Dorn was also masked and had removed his slave's collar. He still wore the harness through which his cock and balls protruded. As Tom watched, the cock began to lengthen, apparently turned on by the prospect of the

19

new slave pinioned for his pleasure.

"What the fuck -?" Tom growled. He was cut short by the stinging back of Steve's hand across his mouth.

"Don't speak until you are given permission, slave," Steve snarled.

Slave??!! Tom's mind reeled. "But - "

Again he swallowed his words as Dorn grasped his cock and balls in one hand and twisted sharply. The sudden pain bent his body as much as permitted by the shackles, and he gasped and choked.

Holding strong pressure on the tortured organs, Dorn gritted, "We said we would help you make up your mind. That means you must experience both sides before you can make a decision. It is your turn to be our slave."

Tom groaned from the crushing of his balls. Dorn gave an additional twist and pulled upward. Tom gritted his teeth and raised his hips, trying to ease the tension, but Dorn maintained the pressure.

"Isn't that right? You may speak now, slave. Isn't that right?"

Tom gasped again. Anything to relieve that pressure. "Yes, yes - "

Again Steve's hand bruised the side of his face with a sudden slap. "That's something else - anything you say will be preceded and followed by a respectful 'Sir', is that clear?"

Tom tasted a trickle of blood from his cheek. The night of leather bliss had turned into a nightmare. Obviously he had no choice but to obey and watch for his chance.

"Yes," he moaned. He saw the hand being raised again to punish his other cheek. "Yes, Sir," he quickly amended. Slowly the threatening fist dropped and the thumb hooked into the wide studded belt around Steve's waist.

"That's better," Steve muttered. "Let up on that meat, Dorn - we don't want to damage the merchandise too severely - yet," he ordered.

Dorn chuckled. "Don't worry about that. Look at the hard-on growing from our gentle ministrations," he sneered. And it was true. Tom suddenly realized that his cock had started its upward surge, perhaps from the rough fist or - something else.

"Get the cat," Steve ordered. Dorn turned to the leather closet and brought out the whip which had given him so much painful pleasure before.

Steve's voice seemed gentler as he spoke to Tom. "You know you like leather, but you don't know what leather is or what leather can do for you. You are about to get a taste of the black friend in my hand." Tom stared at the Master who was caressing the thick leather handle with its cold studs. The narrow leather thongs draped gracefully from his grasp, but the knots in the end of each thong held promise of more than limpid pleasure.

Abruptly Steve swung the whip down, the lashes striking the leather coverlet between Tom's spread legs. Tom jumped, startled but not touched. Steve drew the lashes up over one of Tom's legs slowly, allowing the thongs to ride gently over the muscular, hairy columns. One of the thongs kissed his ball sack as it passed, and Tom shivered from the brief contact. The thongs rose over ridged belly muscles and entwined with the crisp black, curly hair covering Tom's chest. They snaked over his face, giving a brief whiff of sensuous, tangy aroma as they passed.

Again Steve stroked the full length of the tethered body with the lashes. Tom's eyes closed as he felt the spell of the leather tendrils teasing his taut frame. Again the brief touch on his balls. As the nipples were touched they tensed in response. His tongue snaked out to catch one of the lashes as they were drawn across his face.

The next time Steve struck one calf with the whip. Tom jumped slightly but ignored the brief discomfort; he was anxious to feel the thongs caressing his tense muscles and hoping this time the leather would touch his cock with its magic. He did not realize that his cock was standing stiffly upright, throbbing in tempo with his pulse which was increasing gradually as the leather permeated his senses.

Steve directed the teasing thongs over the big balls and around the base of the huge cock pulsing high. Tom tried to move toward the lashes, wanting desperately to prolong the contact with the virile force. His eyes were still closed but he moaned in disappointment as the thongs withdrew from his excited balls. As the lashes snaked over his face, he opened his mouth wide and tried to grasp one of the leather thongs between his teeth, but Steve withdrew the whip.

"He's hungry for it," Dorn murmured.

Steve grunted. "Yes, but he has not yet felt the power. He has no respect, only selfish gratification fills his mind."

He stepped back a pace and brought the whip down with a snap that flicked Tom's left nipple with the tips of the knotted thongs. Tom lurched and howled with the sudden pain but then became quiet, his eyes still closed, his senses tasting the flavor of the leather pain. But before he could thoroughly explore the new sensations the whip descended on the right nipple and he lurched again, his head twisting from side to side, his arms and legs thrashing to the extent they were permitted to move.

The next blow struck his heavy balls resting on the leather cover between his legs. Again he howled from the sudden pain and surprise, and his balls pulled up to his groin, hugging the base of his towering prick. The stinging nipples were forgotten in the face of this new threat to his prized nuts. Again the lash descended with a snap, stinging the wrinkled skin of the hairy sack and surging into his groin and cock with dull hurt. He was beginning to sort out the good from the bad, the stinging slap which could also be a kiss.

Finally he felt the contact he had desired. Steve wrapped the slim thongs around his stiff cock, twisting the leather around the shaft.

"Yes," Dorn hissed, watching the leather kissing the powerful organ. He grasped the throbbing dick enclosed in the thongs, the rough leather cutting into the tense, tender skin under the pressure of his tight fist. He jerked roughly a few times. Tom lurched stiffly, the leather seeming to enter his being and impart an added awakening of lust, his increasing need for orgasm. Sensing his need, Dorn removed his hand. It was too early for that.

He returned to the closet and brought back a single leather thong. He tied a loop in one end and threaded the free end through it. As Steve removed the embracing whip, Dorn dropped the loop of leather around his cock and balls and pulled it tight around them. Again Tom jerked, but this time there was satisfaction in the rough leather contact. Dorn pulled upward experimentally; the leather loop imprisoned the massive rod and tense balls in a sensuous circle, cutting into the flesh, damning the flow of blood out of the throbbing shaft, and slowly turning it purple. The ten-inch prong began to grow even larger.

As Dorn continued to pull, Tom began to writhe and moan, the dull pain spreading from his crotch into his gut. But the pain was mixed with sexual stimulation this time; if only he could reach his cock, jerk it and stroke it as the leather imposed its will! He pulled hard on his bonds, but they were implacable. His cock throbbed stronger and stronger, nodding darkly in the air.

Again the whip snarled down to his aching nipples, stinging and bringing them erect. Tom's leg and arm muscles bulged against the restraints.

Then he felt a golden touch. Dorn's tongue barely touched the tense cockhead. Tom lurched upward, attempting to drive the entire aching shaft into the warm cavern, but Dorn moved back. As Tom sagged, Dorn followed him, teasing the flaring cockhead as he tightened the leather vise still tighter. The wet tip of his tongue followed the ridge of the mushroom, barely flicking the sensitive area and turning Tom into a shuddering mass of desire.

"Please, please - " Tom groaned. In response, Steve brought the cat down with another searing blow to his bruised nipples. Tom lurched violently.

"Please SIR!" Tom shouted, every muscle in his body rigid, his entire being focused on his stiff prick and its demands. His mouth twisted open but his eyes remained closed.

"Here, chew on this!" Steve snarled, and stuffed all the thongs of the cat into Tom's mouth.

At first Tom gagged on the rough whip lashes, but then as his saliva soaked in and he began to savor the bitter essence, he began to suck them greedily. Still Dorn persisted in tantalizing him with his tongue while the leather sank into his flesh and his purple cock and throbbing balls became more and more engorged.

Then Steve snatched the leather thongs from his mouth. Tom dimly realized that, as soon as he grew accustomed or even accepting of a threat, it was taken away and another challenge was presented. After a moment he felt the tension relieved from his legs. Tentatively he lifted one leg and it was free. Then the other one was loose also.

"Hold his legs high, Dorn. Let's see how he likes leather this way!"

Together the tormenters bent both legs back at the knees, bringing Tom's ass up for the first time. Dorn knelt above the prisoner's head and held the muscular legs jack-knifed for Steve's next move.

"That's a nice, trim, solid ass you got there, slave. Let's

see what shape it will be in when we finish with you tonight!" With that he thrust one finger in roughly, through the sphincter and deep into the hot cavern.

Tom had never been fucked, even by a finger. He gasped and lurched with the sudden pain, but then was seized with a burst of intense pleasure as the finger struck a sensitive nerve deep in his body. "Ugghh!" he moaned, completely confused by the mixture of pleasure and pain he was experiencing. Steve thrust back and forth a few times, and with each movement, Tom moaned with increasing pleasure.

Again the finger was immediately removed. He retrieved the whip and held the butt end of the handle at the tiny puckered opening. The steel studs were cold to the sensitive skin. The leather was warm but the handle was impossibly large! Getting fucked with that whip handle would be unthinkable!

Tom's ass muscles tensed, forbidding entry. Although Steve pressed the handle steadily, the muscles refused to relax. Tom's teeth were clenched, any such entry to be resisted.

"Pull harder on that thong around his cock and balls," Steve directed. Dorn held the thong between his teeth and began to tighten the noose again. Immediately Tom cringed from the pain but the tight leather was almost welcome now, bringing his stiff cock to full potency, throbbing powerfully against his rigid belly.

Steve began to soothe the asshole with his fingertips around the leather dildo. At first Tom again resisted, but as Dorn pulled tighter Tom forgot the potential threat to his ass for the real pain and pressure in his staff. A moment later he felt a sudden pain in his asshole - the tip of the handle had penetrated, and his asshole was being stretched as never before! Again he clamped down but that only served to increase the pain. His throbbing dick was forgotten for the moment.

25

Then he felt a soothing touch which eased the pain somehow. Steve's tongue was circling the leather handle, lapping the tight muscles resisting the invader. The combination of the warm leather and the dipping tongue brought shudders to his taut frame. Involuntarily he rolled his ass up for more of that exquisite treatment.

Steve maintained the pressure against his asshole as he rimmed it, and the handle gradually slid deeper and deeper into the virgin ass, lubricated with warm saliva. Even the metal studs disappeared up the channel.

Tom's resistance and then his acceptance of the huge dildo, the virile ass being filled with the studded leather, was intensely exciting to Steve. The leather pouch containing his prick and balls was strained outward by its aroused contents.

"Yes..." Tom hissed unconsciously, "... fill me with leather, that warm, stud leather - ugh, deeper... more... deeper..."

Steve trembled with lust at the sight and smell and taste of the leather dildo entering the stud's asshole. His tongue circled and slurped and the ass muscles relaxed, almost pulling in the dildo now, sucking the leather deeper and deeper inside.

"Hot asshole full of leather, man..." Steve panted, watching Tom writhing uncontrollably around the leather prod. "That's what a man's ass if for..." Tom's mouth was working silently, gasping for air. "Dorn, sit on his face, man. Make him eat your ass while I ream him!"

Tom opened his eyes only to see the sturdy thighs and creamy buttocks move over him and then the shadowed crotch and ass over his face. Eating ass had never been one of Tom's desires, but at that moment he needed asshole to complete the scene. The leather pulling his throbbing dick and the huge leather dildo in his ass were changing his outlook on many things. As the puckered lips above met his straining ones, his resistance disappeared and he enthusiastically kissed the fragrant asshole, beginning to appreciate the significance of the act.

The trim buns which he had fucked so happily settled down over his face. Dorn moaned with increasing pleasure as Tom lapped the sweaty aperture. Steve began to move the dildo in and out slowly, the warm leather and cold metal studs stretching the manly asshole and pushing everything else aside. Steve's tongue darted and lapped around the leather shaft. He shoved in deeper each time, the handle now nearly buried in Tom's gut.

Tom sucked furiously on Dorn's asshole, pushing his stiffened tongue deep into the boy above him, trying to match the penetration by the leather prong. His throbbing prick leaked pre-cum over his belly. He could taste the musk, the inner core of the boy, and could smell the aroma of leather from the harness and the sweaty asshole. More! He wanted more of everything -more leather deep in his gut, more asshole to suck, more manhood to devour!

In frustration he strained at the shackles holding his arms. Most of all now he wanted to pull Dorn's trim body down to his face, to move the beautiful ass as he made love to it, consumed it.

Dorn sensed his need and unsnapped the shackles, freeing his wrists. It was no longer necessary to hold Tom's legs, as he was straining to take more and more of that leather up his ass. Tom grasped Dorn's thighs and pulled them down on his face tightly, burying his face between the trim buns.

Dorn gasped as the thick tongue penetrated deeply, the hairy fists tight around his bulging thighs. Tom could feel the dildo moving swiftly now, the steel studs rasping against the sensitive tissues. "More, more!" he cried silently, the leather filling him, gorging him with its heat and power.

And then it was gone. Steve pulled the leather handle

27

out of his ass, leaving a huge, empty chasm. Tom sobbed from the sudden absence, a vacuum that had never existed before but now was crying to be filled. A moment later, Dorn lifted up also, leaving his gasping mouth slack and empty.

"Oh, please - " he began "Please, Sir - "

"This is what you need - some leather to suck on! Take it!"

Steve shoved the wet dildo into Tom's mouth, the studs striking his teeth, the handle stretching his mouth widely. Tom could smell and taste his own asshole as the dildo was forced into his throat. Dorn held his hands so he could not fight back, but after the first startled moment, there was no resistance. The leather in his mouth was indeed what he needed at the moment; he sucked and lapped it eagerly.

Steve pulled Tom's hips to the edge of the bed and, as Tom lapped the leather joy-stick he shoved his entire prick all the way up the empty asshole with one movement. Tom groaned - in pleasure this time. The hot prick of the leather stud felt even better than the dildo, especially as Steve set up a steady in-and-out rhythm, plowing the stud's ass with long lunges, jabbing the prostate with each stroke.

Dorn moved to Tom's side, tightening the noose around his cock and balls again. Tom's belly was smeared widely with pre-cum, and Dorn could not resist lapping up the sweet juice.

Tom's hot ass was bringing Steve close to climax. Before he reached that point he pulled out and knelt on the floor to shove his tongue far up the channel which he had recently vacated. His tongue probed deeply and his nose nudged the heavy balls just above. He hummed in joy, his face pressed into the manly crotch.

Dorn began to lap Tom's throbbing cockhead again, taking just the tip into his mouth. Tom tensed, his brain steadying for a moment. He saw his chance!

Suddenly he straightened out his legs and trapped Steve's head in a vise-like scissors between his bulging thighs. His sudden turn came as a surprise to both the masked tormenters. Steve tried to squirm out of Tom's grip, but it was no use. And then Tom rolled up and forward, taking Steve with him to the floor. In a split second Tom was on his knees on the floor, Steve's head still clamped between his thighs.

"Now, fucker, let's see how well *you* can suck!" he snarled. He slapped his hard cock against Steve's face mask and then thrust it through the hood's mouth slit into the warmth he needed. He grasped Steve's head in both hands and began to facefuck him mercilessly.

Dorn was so startled he could not react at first. By the time he had recovered his senses, there was no help for Steve. He was being mouth-raped thoroughly by a huge prick long overheated by their own torment.

Steve gagged at first when the huge dick pronged him deeply. He could feel the overdistended veins on the thick shaft, still bulging with blood trapped by the leather thong. The prick was hot and rock-hard, the biggest he had ever had in his mouth. The bulging, hairy thighs held his face tightly in place, the strong hands allowing no escape. Steve, the "super top", was getting face-fucked by the very man he had treated as a slave!

But he was a tremendously exciting man, it was a hugely exciting cock in his mouth, and the hairy chest and masculine face looming above him were enough to compensate for the unaccustomed role he was forced to play. Any guy should be proud to suck that huge prick, take its hot load! And as the thick prick shoved deeply into his throat, he relaxed and sucked it greedily, relishing the virility of the man to whom it belonged.

Tom felt Steve's acceptance of his new submissive role. He felt the smooth tongue caressing the underside of his cock and the lips molding closely to the shaft, the throat welcoming the broad cockhead, and then Steve's hands around his hips, pulling him tighter. A smile formed on Tom's perspiring face and he moaned in joy as the leather stud sucked happily.

Tom turned to Dorn. "Come here, boy," he growled. Dorn came to stand by him, silently acknowledging Tom as a new Master. The trim body in the leather harness and the stiff cock and balls protruding from the jock were enough to bring a decision. Tom pulled him close and literally swallowed his cock, mashing his nose against the leather encircling the stiff meat. The tight balls nudged his chin as he impaled himself on the stiffness and inhaled the heady aroma of leather and man-crotch.

Steve gazed up at the stud fucking his face and sucking off his slave. His brain whirled with unaccustomed lusts, the reversed roles scattering his thoughts wildly. One hand moved to his rigid rod which lurched unattended. He began to jerk it rapidly as he watched the scene above and took that thick cock as far as possible into his throat.

All three men were groaning with rising passions, sweat dripping freely, muscles tense and bulging. The leather mask rasped against Tom's cock, adding to the excitement of face-fucking the leather-stud. And Tom could taste the pre-cum oozing from Dorn's dick; soon they would all be on the verge.

"Oh, God, yeah - " Dorn moaned as he watched the action and gloried in the Master role. "Suck that prick, man! Shove that huge rod into that leather face! Oh, Jesus, are you going to get a load!"

Tom's huge cock was swelling to even greater dimensions as his climax approached. Steve struggled to take it all, frantic for the precious cum he knew was close. And his hand jerked wild and wet, the pre-cum dripping freely from his cockhead.

30

A murmur started in Toms' throat, softly at first, and then growing to a low rumble as the tide began to sweep upward from his groin.

Just then a jet of cum flooded his mouth at the same moment his own flow deluged Steve's slurping mouth below. Tom and Steve avidly gulped down the delicious cream. And then Steve's cock spilled over his hand, gushing white, dribbling to his hairy belly and crotch as he continued to flail away at his dick.

Three hot studs, climaxing together, taking and giving man-to-man, the heady aroma of leather pervading, setting the stage for straining sinews and streaming sweat of shared sensuality.

It was only the beginning of Tom's lust for leather.

THE END

Some say that Masters are made, not born;
one thing I am sure of -
it's a lot of fun making them ...

# THE BLACK BIKER

The morning mist swirled around me as I tightened the crisscross bungie cords over my sleeping bag and ticked off the supplies already loaded on the 750 Honda. Since I wasn't going anywhere special, it wouldn't require much to keep me going for a few days on the road. It was time to get away, I knew, but not to some spa or bar-oriented pseudo-culture most gays seemed to seek out. The sleek, red motorcycle between my legs could do more for that chronic crotch-itch than all the carefully mustached clones transplanted from the Castro.

I zipped up my black leather chaps and jacket, settled my helmet over the mirrored sunglasses, and took a final piss before locking up. Then suddenly remembering, I went back for the *anka*, the Japanese warmer for the sleeping bag, and a few lumps of charcoal useful for keeping warm through the cold nights in the Sierra. I roared off down the street and to the entrance to the Bay Bridge without a backward look at the San Francisco hilltops glittering in the morning sun.

The traffic was light on I-80 since it was well past the usual holiday season, the latter part of September. The wind whistling past my head and the smooth purr of the bike between my legs was enough to start that calming effect I needed, and even the diesel fumes from the trucks smelled good and fresh. I locked the cruise control at 65 mph and drove automatically, my brain refreshingly blank and ready for whatever might happen.

The only thing to catch my eye was another biker stopped beside the highway, apparently tightening the cords on his GoldWing which was loaded similarly to mine. The red scarf around his neck first caught my eye, but the trim buns framed by his chaps also came in for an appreciative glance in the split seconds it took to pass.

I reminded myself that I was getting away from that for at least a few days - just communing with nature and sorting out my thoughts, remember?

But while I was sipping coffee and munching a sandwich at my favorite roadside restaurant near Sacramento, the first stop, the guy showed up again. He sauntered into the restaurant, unwrapping that bright red scarf, and eased onto the counter stool. I couldn't help taking stock of the flashing dark eyes, the slight beard stubble over the strong chin, and the straight black hair needing a trim. The crotch looked packed but with no particular outline, and when he pushed back on the stool while surveying the menu, that enticing ass was even more obvious.

Doggedly I shook my head, deliberately looking away. I had to get my mind off sex if I expected any kind of rejuvenation from this trip, and the guy obviously wasn't gay anyway. Probably there would be a dozen guys just as attractive in the San Francisco bars tonight, but it would end up the same way - zilch. I was getting away from all that. I hurriedly finished my coffee, paid the bill, and was back on the highway in a few minutes.

About twenty miles east of Sacramento I turned off onto country roads and started the gradual climb toward my favorite camping spot near the American River. I almost missed the trail into the woods and had to brake sharply before picking my way around potholes to the little clearing not far from the highway. By the time I had unpacked and had a fire going it was almost dark, but the peace and quiet of the lonely spot had already begun to untangle my nerves. I stripped down and stood nude near the fire, my ass cold from exposure to the night air and my cock warm and thick in the firelight.

It was good to stand there nude with no thoughts of exhibiting myself for another guy, just free and unrestrained. I tensed my leg muscles defined in flickering shadows, my light brown crotch hair glistening, my balls heavy but pulled up against the cold. But my cock seemed to have a life of its own, and stretched out and up as I watched almost with detachment. Soon it was throbbing and thrusting for no apparent reason, and I smiled benignly at it. Well, why not? It's what I usually did on Saturday night anyway these days.

I wrapped my fist around it, covering about half its eight or nine inches, and squeezed it hard. It jerked back at me as if anxious to go, almost the same feeling I got when my bike seemed to strain at the leash when poking along at an easy pace on the highway. Apparently my dick hadn't got the word that I was getting away from all that! But nevertheless my fist started working and it felt so good, my own stiff prick in my hand, all alone in the woods, no one around to see or care.

I stroked long and slow, my knees buckling at times with the sensations flooding my brain and bringing a quiver to my muscles. I closed my eyes, seeing myself in the middle of a leafy vortex, the soft breeze kissing my ass no longer cold but part of the living, pulsating organism whose apex was the throbbing dick in my hand. I rocked back and forth in the isolated glade, oblivious to the sighing of the trees and the faint rustle of the forest around me.

As I spun contentedly, slowly gaining momentum, there came an interruption in the flow of energy about me, an eddy in the otherwise continuous stream. I kept my eyes closed, but I wondered about the sensed but unidentified intrusion. And then a gentle crack, like a footfall on a dead twig, snapped my eyes open with a jerk. Across the fire from me stood the dark, towering figure of the biker I had seen on the highway.

I guess I jerked slightly, my trance invaded by the vision in the black helmet with visor raised, black leather jacket, chaps and boots, the black eyes over the black stubbly chin. Even the scarf looked black in the dim light. The black eyes glistened as they surveyed me and I must have looked strange, a tall, naked blond with my long, hard cock in my suddenly stationary fist. We stared at each other for a long moment, both startled at the encounter but taking stock of each other in that unlikely setting. Then a grin broke the dark countenance, exposing startlingly contrasting white teeth, and he spoke in a deep whisper.

"Sorry to interrupt."

I continued to stare, my head still spinning from the mystical experience but galvanized by the total masculinity and powerful visage of the man across the darting flames. My cock was still rock-hard.

"Saw the glimmer of your fire from the highway and was afraid of a forest fire. Didn't mean to, uh, break in on you."

The dark eyes shifted downward to gaze steadily at my rampant cock.

"Feels good, sometimes, to play with it out here in the open, nobody around to care, just nature for company," he said softly. "Mind if I join you?"

I still remained silent, but watched as the stranger unbuttoned his fly and extracted a thick piece to match my own. A few strokes and it was at full staff, the dark, bulging cockhead partly capped with delicate foreskin which withdrew as the fist began to stroke it slowly.

I watched in fascination as the black biker set up a rhythm, and without realizing it, I began to stroke my own in perfect synchrony. Our eyes locked, occasionally moving to focus on the prick in the other's hand, noting the glistening pre-cum moistening the bulging cockheads, and back to the eyes blue and black, intense and searching.

Instinctively we moved a step closer to each other, standing close to the low fire that toasted our pendulous

36

balls rocking gently in their hairy sacks. The black leather whispered softly as the biker's arm moved, and the firelight cast glimmers and reflections in the black helmet and steel studs.

Unconsciously we leaned forward until the cockheads almost touched, our gazes bonded as our bodies seemed to blend in a single space in nature's setting. The black and the light, the dark and the blond, so different and yet so similar, two men sharing identical emotions, total understanding, as part of nature's design.

Barely missing a stroke, my hand moved the few inches required to replace the biker's hand on his throbbing lance. The dark hand moved away reluctantly, a question appearing in the dark eyes. But the question was there for only a moment, acceptance replacing it without reservation. And then the hand with the bristling black hairs moved to grip my blond cock, so like his own but different, to match the increasing rhythm. Then it was my turn to grin as the biker's hand brought even greater urgency to the growing demands of my cock and I felt an equal response in the dark cock throbbing in my grip.

Mutual excitement swelled as we grinned at each other, our breathing taking on a spasmodic quality. We were on a mutual excursion to a known but mysterious place. We had never been there before, not like this, not together, not with nature's wildness as a third party. But we knew it was right, it was inevitable, and we would experience together what had always been solitary. We were aware of each quiver, each gasp, each vestige of tension in the other, and automatically adjusted to enhance the connection.

I could hear our muscles snap rigidly as we neared our completion, each leaning toward the other, our hands flying on threatening pricks moist with pre-cum. Without conscious thought, I leaned forward and placed my lips on those of my noctural lover.

At first there was no response. There was no definite withdrawal, but the unaccustomed contact was apparently confusing to the black biker. To me it was the obvious missing element in this mind-boggling experience, but it was clearly new to him. But then gradually passivity was replaced with acceptance, stillness with trembling, and the sharing of the passion we both felt was confirmed. His leather arm clasped me close, the dark lips pressing strongly so that I had to twist my head to fit the space available through the face opening of the black helmet.

Both cocks lurched strongly in our flailing fists and, as our tongues probed deeply, both pricks shot streams of whiteness over their counterparts. We groaned into each other's mouths as we pumped our milky messages to each other, coating each other with the sticky essences of man, the drippings hissing and crackling in the fire below. Streams of iridescent whiteness marked the union of black and blond alone in the wilderness. And even after the emission had dwindled to an ooze, we continued to milk and stroke each other, reluctant to end the magic moment.

I was first to pull away, curious of the black biker's reaction, but the dark eyes were clouded, apparently wrestling with unfamiliar thoughts. But then the grin reappeared and he looked down, his hand dropping away slowly from my dribbling cock.

"Wow," he said softly and looked away into the darkness.

"Yeah," I breathed, not really wanting or daring to talk.

The biker flipped his cock once and then tucked the softening rod into his pants. "Guess I had better get going," he sighed.

He couldn't leave now, I thought frantically, please! But I stifled that before I suggested calmly that the biker share my sleeping bag. The man stared at me for a moment and then shrugged, "OK, I guess it would be warmer that way," with another smile.

I watched as he wheeled the GoldWing closer to the fire and set it for the night with a flat stone under the kickstand. The biker moved with a grace that was almost animalistic, and the bike was an element of the man that seemed to blend into the scene without disturbance of the nature around them.

I stirred finally and placed a lump of charcoal into the dying fire. When it was hot I managed with a stick to place it in the hollow of the *anka*. I unrolled the sleeping bag and placed the closed warmer in the foot end. When I looked up, the biker had removed his clothes and I saw him naked for the first time. He was rangy and trim, his broad chest covered with more of the bristly black hair that made him so striking, and a thick black bush framed his still long, swinging prick.

"Guess we had better douse this," he said, scuffing dust over the dying embers until the fire was out. We were suddenly even more alone in the darkness with only intermittent moonlight filtering through the tree branches above.

I was suddenly embarrassed for some reason, and slid swiftly into the sleeping bag. A moment later the long, lank form of the biker joined me, his skin seeming almost hot to the touch at first, the hairy legs stretched out beside mine. The biker zipped up the bag and we were clasped together in the darkness.

"Foot warmer makes it real cosy," the biker murmured. "Yeah," I agreed, and then all was silent.

I lay quietly, thinking. The guy was probably straight, based on his hesitancy during their strange experience at the fire, but still not resistant, that was for sure. I was still a little shaken from the intensity of it all, but decided I had better cool it, not rock the boat. I turned away from the biker to show that I wasn't expecting anything, and a moment later the biker also turned on his side within the close confines of the sleeping bag. Our asses kissed and it felt so great I almost pressed against him, but instead tried to remain apart as much as possible.

It was snug there with this unknown hunk, this mysterious stranger out of the darkness. I was strangely content, even though I did not even know his name. Our sex had been very satisfying and I should leave it at that. I drifted off to sleep quickly despite the strange circumstances.

It was probably several hours later that I awoke to the probings of a very large stiff prick between my buns. It felt so good, so promising, that I moved sleepily toward my "mate" without thinking. Then I remembered where I was and tried to move away again. This time I was prevented, not so much by the sleeping bag but the brawny arm clasped around my chest.

Then I felt soft lips and a bristly chin on my shoulder, and my pulse rose as my cock awoke. The biker said nothing but kissed my shoulders and neck as his free hand explored the rest of my now trembling body. The calloused fingers roved over my legs and ass, moved to my chest to thumb the tiny nipples, and finally moved down to grip my rod rigid against the sleeping bag. The thick cock filled my ass crack, the curly black pubic hairs caressing me from behind.

I writhed and moved under the touch, responding immediately to each nuance, willing the biker to do whatever he wished, take whatever he wanted. It was a surrender more total than I had ever before allowed myself. There had been times when I had thought I was surrending to another guy, but I had always held something back, I realized at that moment. This time was different. I knew that the black biker was my master and could demand anything of me, knowing I would submit totally and completely. I felt myself grow limp and receptive except for my throbbing dick. I was trembling with desire but afraid to move for fear of breaking the spell.

The arm gripped me strongly, and I felt the bristly chest hairs grinding against my back. The biker's breathing was faster, his body pressing harder and twisting against me. And I knew he also felt my surrender, even though no words were spoken.

I felt the cockhead at my asshole, begging for admittance. There was no question. I adjusted my body for what I knew would be the ultimate invasion, and almost immediately I felt the slow, gentle entry of the huge cock into my longing tunnel. It was painful at first, but that was as it should be. Only as the pain was relieved by fullness and acceptance of my role of slave would our relationship be established.

The thick prick moved in, slowly, deliberately, inexorably, opening me wide. The biker gripped my cock and balls in an iron fist, possessively and almost painfully, but that was as it should be. I belonged to him and the biker knew it. His stiffness advanced inward, spreading me, filling me with heated manhood that could not be denied. And when the bristly crotch hairs grated my asshole, when the hairy balls kissed me firmly, I knew that was where I belonged. He gripped my throbbing prick in his hairy fist, mute evidence of submissive passion previously denied.

The biker began to move rhythmically, almost hypnotically, establishing his dominance over and over, and I moaned as the fullness pervaded my deepest instincts. The strokes grew longer, all the way in and almost all the way out, each thrust a promise and an assertion of our togetherness. And with each movement, I approached closer and closer to a nirvana that I sensed matched the tide in my master.

The man began to thrust harder and deeper, no longer

gentle but insistent and demanding, taking what was his, knowing he would not be denied. I moved in full reciprocity, needing that insistent hammering, welcoming the repeated invasion because it allowed me to submit repeatedly, thrilling to the new clarity in my life. His grip of my cock and balls was excruciating but added to the passion beginning to crest.

With a grunt, the biker thrust deeper than before, and I felt the throbbing, spasming victory deep in my gut. I was almost unaware that my own prick was gushing whitely in the grip of my master. My entire body was climaxing from head to toe, matching the enormity of my master's supremacy.

It seemed to last for hours, that soaring, searing trip to nowhere and everywhere in the arms of my lover. It was unbearable pain mixed with unbearable pleasure, and I wished it would never stop. But finally the stars settled in their positions, the moon again shone sweetly through the treetops, and the world was right side up again.

The last thing I remembered before falling asleep again was his soft lips on my neck...

When I awoke in the morning there was no sign of the biker. The sleeping bag was zipped up neatly, but I was alone in it. I scrambled up and checked for the GoldWing, but there was no strange bike or even any signs that another bike had been there.

But as I rolled up my sleeping bag to resume my journey, there was a very damp spot where my cock had rested during the night.

THE END

# A DANGEROUS PLACE

I first saw him sagging against the wall of the empty elevator, his eyes glassy and far off, his faded levis patched and grimy, his sneakers scuffed and close to falling apart. He was a prime target.

My instincts told me that my night wasn't over yet. My lids were heavy but there was one more scene to do on this theatrical night in that city overpowered by the theatrical and hyped-up mundane. The clamor from the street revelers reached me in blasts in that hotel lobby each time the doors swung open to admit another couple or group, all exhausted, draped with strings of silly beads and trinkets tossed from floats and driven by mass hysteria like I was. They were piling up behind me as I blocked the elevator door. Six foot two with broad shoulders in full leather can intimidate even George and Suzie from Memphis who would be teaching Bible school again next week after their sodden trip to the Mardi Gras.

He didn't really look at me, not then. He was gazing at something else, perhaps a memory, perhaps a fantasy, but it didn't matter. He was a piece of humanity that I could use to impose my will, make him eat shit. Without moving from the door, I touched the "Close" button, shutting out all those chattering tourists.

He still didn't respond as we ascended to my floor. He took in the black vision of death and punishment without a flicker of resentment or fear. It was all the same to him. His plaid shirt was open almost to the navel, the buttons gone, and the liberal clustering of brown chest hair matched the curls on his head. His chin showed scatterings of stubble that hadn't seen a razor recently. The blue eyes seemed hypnotized by the red "On" light on the elevator panel.

There were lots of guys like him in New Orleans,

college students mostly, who went from bar to bar, bed to bed, or maybe got sucked off in the alley a few feet away from a piano pounding out blues. Sometimes the rising scream of a saxophone coincided with the orgasmic climax, leaving them uncertain if they had dreamed it or if it had been only a momentary interruption in their euphoria.

It was Sunday night, or early Monday morning, I think; at least it was after the Bloody Marys at Lafitte's and the Hurricanes at Pat's. We all took whatever was available. Leathermen, aging faggots, teeny boppers, blacks, whites, Cajuns, straight and gay, hesitant and flamboyant, we jammed the streets and alleys and courtyards under French lattices. Our schedules were all pretty much the same but did not often coincide exactly. The days and nights were episodes of seeming clarity with parades down Canal and Bourbon Streets every few hours and always with a drink in our hands. The streets were already a foot deep in plastic cups and occasionally broken glass bottles, forbidden but there just the same. When we saw a crowd we would barge into the middle of it, just to feel the hands over our bodies and groping our leather crotches; sometimes the hands belonged to frizzyhaired matrons whose dreary husbands were too drunk to get it up. And when it got hard we would head for a gay bar where we knew the masses of guys high on whatever drove them would envelope us in nudging shoulders while someone knelt between our boots, his mouth warm and succulent.

But then we would return to our beds for a few hours and try to recover sufficiently for the next parade, the next shot in the arm. We would return to the streets and the bars and the alleys, never disappointed because the rerun crowd was still there, revitalized from their own few hours of respite.

When the door opened the floor was silent as a tomb.

A faint light from the end of the hall suggested a dawn that had not yet made up its mind.

My gloved hand around his neck pushed him down the hall, and he stumbled a little on the worn carpeting. When we reached my door I grabbed his shirt collar to stop him or he would have continued down the hall into that hazy grayness. I fumbled the door open and pushed him through it. He landed on his knees by the bed, not a bad place to begin.

I leaned against the closed door, watching him, but he merely stared at the floor, as if viewing a landscape etched in silver like those on easels in Jackson Square. I had left on the bathroom light, and it was enough. I stripped off my gloves, sweaty and stiff, as I watched him and surveyed the young ass with crack showing above the levis. Another slave to ravage. Another body to prove my mastery over. On his knees, of course.

I slapped it hard with my gloves, but he didn't grunt. Good. I wanted to rip off those levis, but had the sense to know that he needed at least a top button. I reached under his belly and unfastened it, then tore them down. The white roundness showed he was not a beach boy, although he had that kind of body. He was hairless but his asshole was reddened, a green light to me in my mood.

Even when I entered him he made no sound. Didn't he know I needed resistance, some sign of chagrin at being stuffed full? I knelt behind him, my leather crotch pressed intermittently against him, and he merely braced himself silent and unresponsive. After a few more strokes I pulled out - not much fun after all.

Instead I sat on the edge of the bed, my battered erection still game for more, and pulled him forcibly over on it. His mouth opened dumbly and accepted his assignment with its intimate odor. When he didn't move beyond that point, I pushed him down, then up, insisting on my due.

For the first time his eyes focused on my face, his throat stuffed, as if trying to associate my face with my prick. His blue eyes searched my dark ones, perhaps wondering if he had been there before, or if he could recognize me from some previous episode in the midst of revelry and debauchery. I snarled at him, but it made no difference. He was going to make me work for it, it seemed.

Growing bored with his passivity, I facefucked him, holding his curly head until I disgorged my frustration. He swallowed automatically. Immediately I was bone-weary. I lay back on the bed and then moved up to the pillow without undressing. I found my cap on the floor beside the bed the next morning.

Some time during that few hours of sleep I awoke enough to realize that he had crawled on the bed beside me, his limbs entangled with my leather ones, and I think he kissed my chest.

The sound of drums and whistles penetrated the old walls of the hotel. It was morning and somebody-or-other was strewing silly medals and beads into the drunken crowds on Royal Street. Monday, the day before the big one. I buried my head under the pillow, not able to face the sunshine streaming around the shade, but the sounds persisted. I felt his warmth next to me.

I felt clammy in my leather jacket and pants, and my boots had left muddy smudges on the cheap gray coverlet. Lafitte's was probably jammed by now, the Bloodys-with-the-beef-broth cocktail pouring down throats parched from whiskey and smoke and trying to talk over the din that was everywhere. And to top it off, somebody was pounding on the door - the maid, I suppose. I growled something and she went away.

When I finally surfaced his eyes were fixed on mine. They had little flecks of brown. I didn't want to see clear eyes with questions in them. I shut my eyes. He didn't

46

move.

"Undress me," I ordered, but had to clear my throat before the words came out with authority. I kept my eyes closed while he struggled with the boots and the damp socks. I raised up enough for him to slip the jacket over my shoulders. It took him a while to figure out the buckle on my studded belt, and then I could feel his uncertainty about the method of getting my pants off. Eventually he stripped them off like a glove so they ended up inside out, but I was a dead weight for him to move around.

"Tongue bath," I ordered shortly, my words muffled by the pillow. He showed his experience by starting at my toes and working up, but he missed a few spots.

"Kiss my ass," I growled when he had reached my shoulders. I knew he didn't like that - a master can tell - but he did it. And when I turned over, my boner slapped his face.

This time he took it like a man, or maybe he was just hungry. He was playing with himself and I cuffed his hand away.

I took him in the shower with me and instructed him how to bathe a man. Once in a while his shiny blues would search my face, not so much looking for approval but in a wondering way. I ignored the unspoken questions.

He watched while I shaved. I caught the beginnings of a smile as I trimmed my mustache and beard.

When we reached the street I patted him on the shoulder and started down the street. Something made me turn around, and he was walking slowly toward me, his eyes moist. I shook my head and lost myself in the crowd.

I ran into him again that night. The whole she-bang of Mardi Gras takes place within a dozen square blocks or so, so that's not unusual. It was the lighting up of his face when he saw me that was unusual.

I had just left a raunchy Spanish bar, I remember. The music was mostly maracas, the drinks were either beer or tequila, and all the guys had girls in peasant blouses with them. But the same guys stood patiently in line in the back to watch or to suck or get sucked off by whomever was in the mood, and there were always plenty who were.

I was in a good mood, the kind that flies high before it crashes. I didn't even swing at the guy who bumped me and knocked my cap askew; the guy's fly was open and his dong was half out, but nobody cared. The blue eyes came at me like a laser from the darkness.

He stood tall and straight, the fuzz gone and with a more or less clean polo shirt. His thumbs were hooked in his pockets as he leaned against the dirty brick wall.

I don't usually repeat, you know. Why bother, when practically every guy is available and happy to get on his knees for a stud? But there was something about him - maybe I had missed a secret source of energy that seemed to radiate from him.

I placed a leather arm around his shoulders and his face seemed to glow. His own arm encircled my waist and I was ready to pull away but he pulled me toward the hotel instead. I went along for a while as he chatted to me about some dumb parade or something. He even gave me his name - Steve Komaranski or something like that. The booze kept me a couple of feet off the ground. Before I knew it we were in my hotel lobby and he had pushed the button for the elevator.

I started to pull away but just then the door opened and he almost pulled me in. When the door closed he put his arms around me, resting his head on my chest. I guess I was getting softhearted.

In the room he undressed me as I stood in the middle of the floor. It was almost as if we were equals, and he was a clerk in a men's store or something. Still I didn't toss him out on his can.

"Now you can undress me." He just smiled. I was hard, although I don't know why. I yanked the polo shirt over his head, making his jaws snap shut from the constricting neck, and started to rip off his levis, but he backed away and stepped out of them himself. I was getting mad.

I guess he noticed my expression. He dropped to the floor and started servicing me, and my legs began to tremble. His hands and his mouth were all over me, and before I knew it I was stretched out on the bed like a fuckin' Cleopatra. I pushed him off and got him around the neck but he just giggled and slipped free. I guess my heart wasn't really into it. We wrestled until we got caught in the snarled covers. I got his arm twisted behind him but he wriggled out of the hold, managing to go down on me in spite of my bulk. Tough little fucker!

Just as I was going to give him the real heave-ho he stuck a bottle of poppers under my nose. I don't use it much, and the rush hit me hard. He wrapped his arms around me and as I groaned he stuck his dick in my mouth. It was fat and juicy, and my head floated up to the ceiling. It was only moments before we were swimming in sticky sweetness.

Then he was all obedience and on his best behavior. I couldn't keep my eyes open. I turned away from him. He put his arm under my head and held me close, but I went to sleep anyway.

The next morning I was really pissed off. I had missed at least four hours of action because of this Polish twerp. I punished him by showering alone and he showered while I shaved. When he came out of the bathroom I was dressed in fresh leathers and was ready for him.

"This is Mardi Gras day and you're going to be my slave, kid."

I cut the ass out of his levis with my pocket knife and

made him put them on, checking for the correct exposure. I put my collar around his neck and tightened it almost painfully, then attached a dog chain to the ring. I yanked him out of the room and down to the street. He had a shit-eating grin on his face until I forced him down on his knees as I surveyed the crowd.

The restaurant wasn't very busy, but smelled of spaghetti and sausage. I managed to get some eggs and ordered a sausage for him kneeling on the floor at my feet. All the clods from Des Moines were staring at us, of course. We ignored them. When the Polish sausage arrived I stuffed it in his face. It reminded me of his dick.

All day we sauntered around the Quarter, through crowds of transvestites giggling and flirting, until they saw the dog. Everyone had some sort of stupid mask on, monsters or animals or red-wigged sluts, living the life they loved. Lots of bare ass on weight lifter bodies or ballerinas covered from head to toe. And all day he was the perfect man, not losing his cool, not complaining about anything, no matter what I put him through. He watched me getting a blow-job in a john on Rampart, that calm, composed expression never leaving his face. I let him hold it while I pissed and some guy was eating my ass in the Corral. When we walked down the street he was erect and almost handsome, keeping a half step behind me. I rarely spoke to him except to give an order.

In the afternoon I fed him a Po-Boy and gave him a beer. We watched a whore blowing a wino on Bourbon Street. Everyone cheered when he finally came.

The leather men were all there in full flower, some with slaves in tow, but none of them could come close to mine. I noticed their covetous eyes, but they knew better than to butt in on us. He paid them no attention, walking straight and tall and proud. When he knelt at my feet, his balls showing also, some of the leather studs sometimes nudged his bare ass with a boot, but he ignored it like a man. That night I allowed him to eat a steak and baked potato with me in a little cellar restaurant I particularly liked. I shared my joint with him afterward.

I took him into the orgy room in the back of B.J.'s about midnight. It was fragrant with leather and piss. As instructed, he crouched beside me as slave after slave slobbered over my meat, watching attentively but not interfering. But I wasn't in the mood for some reason. The only time he took a decisive action was when I started to give my piss to some anonymous figure; he nudged the guy out of the way and took it himself. He took it like a man.

We returned to the hotel. He walked beside me and I didn't complain. I had neglected the chain, so he carried it himself. My head was fuzzy - kind of soft in the middle, somehow.

When we got to the room he had me sit in the one easy chair while he stripped. He removed the collar and I didn't complain. He had a good chest and shoulders, and the muscles played as he removed the ruined levis. The light brown fuzz on his legs seemed to glow in the faint light from the bathroom, the muscles tensing and relaxing as he showed off his body. His ass was sunburned from the unaccustomed exposure.

He came close, his hips jerking with the rock on the local station. His cock began to grow, thrusting upward like his breakfast, and then it was in my mouth. He removed my cap and put it on his head, and I looked up at him, those blue lasers cutting through the mist. His balls were hairless and rolled easily in my fingers.

Then he pulled away and sat on the bed, beckoning. I stood up and hurried out of my leathers, my head even fuzzier and hearing a crazy disco beat. When I approached the bed he moved over, but I settled my weight gently on him, bringing his lips to mine. I drank deeply of him, our tongues touching and twisting together. At times I opened my eyes but was burned with the intensity of his gaze that cut through the crust like a torch.

When he pulled away I tried to stop him, but he moved down my body with a flickering tongue until he reached my apex. He tongued it briefly but then moved down, lifting my legs to his shoulders. I lay passive, my brain at a crossroads. And when he entered me it was with a tenderness that banished all other thoughts from my confused brain.

I don't remember whether I came that night or not. I just remember holding him closely, nibbling his ear, kissing his eyelids, a blossoming warmth enveloping us. And eventually we fell asleep that way, the noisy revelers outside retreating to a world that was not ours.

I had to catch my plane back to Chicago that noon. I didn't know what to say to him in the morning. He ruffled my hair as I sat on the bed, putting on my socks. I reached for his cock but he turned away. I tried to say something, I wasn't sure what, but he walked into the bathroom and shut the door. When he came out I was putting on my levis, but he stopped me, handing me the gabardine slacks and loafers I had worn down on the plane straight from work.

As I dressed he wrapped his shirt around his butt and put his levis on over them, covering up effectively if not very subtly. I still wanted to say something, something that would be a link, a tie - but he ignored me. He held the door as I struggled alone with my suitcases full of leather. His face never lost that composed, almost remote expression.

Just before the driver put my biggest bag into the cab, he opened it and removed my steel-rimmed cap. He put it on his head at a jaunty angle, his bare chest broadening with the symbolism. He shook my hand goodbye as if I were a long-lost cousin returning home after a casual visit.

And as the cab pulled away, he saluted carelessly with a broad smile.

New Orleans can be a dangerous place, especially during Mardi Gras.

THE END

Sometimes love creeps in
where even Masters fear to tread -
especially during the madness of Mardi Gras.

# RANCHER'S CHOICE

Kirk checked the corral for the third time for Johnny's horse, but it still wasn't there. The young cowboy was now a half-day overdue from his fence-mending job on Kirk's ranch, but that wasn't the only reason for Kirk's anxiety, he realized. He met his foreman's inquisitive gaze a little defensively.

"You been checking something out here just about every hour," Juan said. "What the hell you worried about?"

"Johnny. He should have been home this morning, I figure. That fence run along the highway shouldn't take any longer than that to repair," Kirk answered shortly.

He didn't mean to bitch at Juan, God knows. Juan was not only his foreman but his best friend, and the only one who had any knowledge of Kirk's recently-discovered homosexuality. But even he didn't know how Kirk felt about Johnny, the young Indian that Kirk had recently added to the ranch crew. He didn't realize that Kirk's cock stirred and lengthened down his worn levis every time he even came close to Johnny, especially when his shirt was off and all that smooth, copper skin was exposed, or when he bent over a task that tightened his levis over his taut, round ass. All he knew was that Kirk was gay and was having trouble adjusting to it, natural enough for a guy who hadn't come out until he was thirty years old.

Juan leaned against a fence post and studied his boss quizzically. "You talkin' as boss and owner, or - somethin' else?"

Kirk looked away into the distance, avoiding the knowing eyes. "Well, he is overdue, and I guess I - shit, I don't know - but every time I'm around him I get all - kind of flustered - wanting to touch him... But he just looks kind of confused and avoids me, it seems."

55

"Well, look, you're his boss, ya know? Even if he is turned on, he sure wouldn't show it for fear of gettin' kicked off the ranch. 'Specially with your reputation as a whore master in the old days," he finished with a grin.

Kirk grinned sheepishly, remembering the night Juan had encountered him in the parking lot of the local whore house, drunk and depressed, knowing he was missing something in life but not able to admit what it was. Juan had showed him the facts of life that night and had acted as a sort of gay father to him in the few brief encounters he had had since then.

Kirk sobered suddenly, his mind made up. He strode to the stable and started saddling his favorite horse. Juan followed.

"Ya goin' after him?" he pressed. "It's almost dark, dangerous for a horse on the range, and you probably couldn't see him even if he was hurt or somethin'."

"I can't help it, Juan, I gotta find him. It's gettin' dark for him, too, ya know."

Juan gave a low whistle and his pie-faced sorrel came cantering over. "You're not goin' alone. I'm comin' along."

Darkness came quickly as they picked their way across the rolling range country. It seemed forever until the moon rose, and even then scattered clouds scuttled across the sky intermittently blocking its silver rays. They eventually stopped on a small hill, hoping the clouds would clear, and contemplated their next move.

"Tell me about Johnny," Juan said simply as they scanned the darkness.

Kirk sighed, not embarrassed but uncertain of how to put his feelings into words. "I guess I love him but I can't talk to him about it. I guess I still haven't accepted the idea of loving another man, so I try to ignore the problem. I suppose I just end up confusing myself and him."

"He may feel the same way and doesn't know how to

react," Juan said softly. "Has it occurred to you that Johnny may have left the ranch because of this conflict between you, and isn't just 'missing' at all?"

Kirk moaned. "Yeah, it occurred to me, and I don't deserve any better, but I don't think he's like that. I think he would come to me straight and not just sneak away. He's proud..."

And then he saw it as he distractedly peered into the darkness - first just a flicker - there it was again!

"There's a fire there, maybe a mile away! Come on, Juan - it may be Johnny!"

As they rode in that direction, they lost sight of the fire intermittently as small hills or tree clumps blocked the view, but eventually they came close enough to see the campsite. Two horses were tethered near the fire under a small grove of trees. But what caught their eyes was the naked figure hanging from a low tree branch and another naked man with a horsewhip in his hands.

Kirk started forward. Juan grabbed his shoulder and pulled him back.

"That must be Johnny!" Kirk protested.

"Maybe it is, but we got to know what we're gettin' into! For Johnny's sake we got to stay calm until we know what we're up against!" Kirk quieted reluctantly; all he could think of was Johnny and what must be happening to him.

"Follow me!" They circled around to a vantage spot in the trees where they were able to see clearly.

As they peered from their place of concealment, the naked form swung the whip to encircle the tied body, and the victim emitted a low scream of pain. His wrists were tied high to a branch which forced him to teeter on tiptoe so he could not resist the repeated attacks of the tall blond man swinging the whip. Stripes were visible on the chest, back, and legs of the smooth, lithe Indian body that Kirk desired so much.

The torturer slashed down with the whip across Johnny's back. The Indian's prick was rock-hard, jutting out sharply; when the whip descended, the cock gave a lurch, becoming even stiffer and larger. Around his cock and balls there were leather straps studded with steel barbs that glistened in the light from the fire.

Again the whip slashed across the bronzed back, and again the hanging, limp figure jerked and the cock swelled even more. It looked almost purple from prolonged erection, and even the balls were tense and swollen. Then the savage attacker dropped the horsewhip and walked to the fire.

Kirk could only concentrate on Johnny who was silent, his head hanging slack, his back and shoulder muscles quivering in the dim light, exhausted from the strain of the torture. The man at the fire picked up a glowing object and started for Johnny, his rigid rod swinging as he moved, but stopped abruptly as he heard the approaching rancher and his foreman.

"Cal! Put that branding iron down!" Juan shouted as he ran toward him. He and Kirk stopped just inside the circle of light from the fire.

The man stared at the intruders, his grip on the glowing branding iron beginning to waver.

"Who is it?" he growled, and then his face grew ashen. "Juan - it's you, isn't it? Is it really you?"

"That's right, Cal, your master is back. You didn't think you would be deprived of your master forever, did you?" Juan's voice was rough, insolent, demanding. He was a different person, suddenly, than Kirk had known before.

"So you've got yourself a slave now? He doesn't really accept you though, does he?" Juan was taunting, sarcastic. "You're no master, Cal, you're my slave and always will be my slave, isn't that right, Cal?"

Cal began to shake violently and he dropped the

branding iron with a thud. His body sagged as Juan strode closer to him, and then he fell to his knees, his hands clasped in supplication.

"Oh, Sir, I didn't mean to displease you but I thought - please, Juan - Master - please - allow me to make amends."

Kirk was totally confused by all this but his only concern was Johnny! Putting aside his many questions, he dashed to Johnny hanging limply in the firelight. His back was criss-crossed with welts from the horsewhip that Cal had used with such force, but the young man's cock was still stiffly protruding and bobbing with frustration and denied release. The dark eyes were closed, not even aware of Kirk's presence.

"Johnny!" Kirk moaned and lifted the semi-conscious form to release the tension on his wrists. The silken, bronze skin of his muscular arms with their quivering muscles was hot to the touch. Kirk wrapped a strong arm around the firm buttocks, lifted the limp body high enough to loose the bonds, and eased him gently to the ground. At least he was alive. The sensual lips hung slack, but as Kirk soothed the sweaty hair tendrils from his face, the eyes opened slowly, dazed and blank.

With shaking hands he unfastened the tight cock-straps, releasing the dammed up blood from the engorged cock and swollen balls. The color lightened to a dull red, but the cock remained rigid, throbbing in its need to erupt.

"Thought you could make a slave out of Johnny by force, did you? Brand him, to make him your property forever? Is that what you were planning, Cal?"

Kirk hardly recognized the cringing torturer in his present role. "Oh, sir, if I could only serve you, my master, I would not need... I saw him from the highway, those beautiful muscles gleaming - I thought... Won't you let me serve you, sir?" he moaned, groveling to Juan on his knees. He began to lick the grimy boots of the foreman as the rugged man towered over him.

"You're not fit to clean my boots!" Juan growled, shoving him away. "I discarded you weeks ago as my slave because of your snivelling weakness, and now you're back tormenting one of my friends. You are unworthy of being called a slave!"

"You're right, sir, but please, *please*, give me another chance - " He groped upward, squeezing and fondling the thick calves and massive thighs of the cowboy as he continued to lick the dusty boots. Juan stood motionless, his face stony and impassive. But when the grasping hands approached the crotch, bulging with manhood, Juan swung and rocked the slave to the ground.

"I didn't tell you you could touch my cock!" he snarled. He drove a booted foot into Cal's exposed crotch, the big cock mashing painfully under the boot.

Cal groaned and doubled up, but then immediately returned to licking the dirty boots. "Sorry, sir," he mumbled. But Kirk could see Juan's cock lengthening down his leg in a hard ridge.

"On your feet, slave!" Juan barked.

Cal scrambled to his feet and stood, head bowed, waiting for the next command. His blond hair caught reddish glints from the fire. His broad shoulders tapered to a narrow waist, and the same reddish-blond hair also matted his chest, continuing downward to surround a thick prick standing at rigid attention.

"What do you want, Cal?" Juan snarled.

"Your cock, sir," Cal whispered.

"What? Speak up!" Juan roared.

Cal jumped to comply. "Your cock, sir - please, sir -" he shouted toward the moon.

Slowly Juan unbuttoned his shirt and removed it. His massive, hairy chest fascinated Cal. He worshipped his master with his eyes. His hand closed over his throbbing prick.

"Get your hand away from that!" Juan snapped. "I will tell you when and if you can touch yourself, pig!"

"Yes, sir," Cal snatched his hand away. His head hung meekly, his arms at his sides. The fire crackled softly and flared up momentarily as a small log moved. The flare accentuated the deep-set eyes fixed on his master's boots. Kirk and Johnny watched and waited tensely.

"Unfasten my belt!" Juan ordered gruffly.

Cal fumbled with the buckle, awkward in his haste. When he finally had it loose, he started unbuttoning the fly, anxious for the thick meat throbbing there. Juan lashed out, leaving a welt on the slave's face, since he had not given permission. Gradually, step by step, the foreman allowed the cringing cowboy to lower his levis and finally to extract the prize, but still he was only allowed to look.

"That's what you want, isn't it, Cal," he sneered. "You don't want Johnny or any other guy to serve you - you just need my big prick, don't you? You're a fuckin' cocksucker, my cock sucker, my ass-licker, and my slave if I'll have you, right, Cal?" His voice rose in a crescendo and Cal whimpered his agreement as the voice rolled over him.

"Show Kirk and Johnny how you can suck cock, slave."

"Oh, yes, sir," Cal mumbled gratefully, immediately falling to his knees and gobbling most of the thick staff into his mouth. He moaned with joy as he sucked hard, greedy for that of which he had been deprived, his eyes closed. Juan watched critically with cool detachment, but Kirk and Johnny could detect a subtle bending of his knees, a softening of his expression, as he was fully engulfed in the hot mouth. Kirk's cock throbbed to full erection in his levis, and Johnny's hand dropped to his own tortured tool still unsatisfied. The young man was kneeling on the ground, his arms around Kirk's legs,

61

reality returning gradually.

Juan pulled back suddenly, making a popping sound as his cock swung free. "Stay where you are, slave," he growled, and the three men's eyes followed his actions closely. Juan brought his and Kirk's horse near the fire and tied the lariat hanging from each saddle to the horns. He tied Cal's wrists to each rope and used his special whistle only his horse understood. Slowly the horse backed away, pulling the ropes tight until Cal was lifted to his feet, his arms stretched painfully between the two horses. The horse stopped as the resistance increased, but the strain was intense as evidenced by Cal's tortured expression. Juan approached his slave again.

"How do you like to be strung up, Cal? Huh? Not much fun, huh? I'll give you somethin' to take your mind off the pain, asshole!"

Juan lowered his levis again and lifted Cal's legs over his arms. His massive hairy thighs bulged with the added weight. His cock pointed directly at the slave's asshole with its sprinkling of red hair, the man suspended by the ropes from the horses.

"You're goin' to get what you really want, your master's prick up your shit-chute, even though you don't deserve it!" With a lunge he forced his dry cock directly into the quivering frame, and it was Cal's turn to scream.

Johnny gripped Kirk's legs hard as he watched the rape of his torturer, and he began to stroke his swollen cock. It was painful, but that was what he wanted at that moment.

Kirk stared in disbelief, unaccustomed to the connection between pain and pleasure that was evident on Cal's face. After his first involuntary outburst, his face creased with smiles as his master scraped and thrust into his hungry ass. It was obvious to Kirk that these men actually enjoyed each other, their love brutal but totally satisfying to both of them, the violence adding to their pleasure.

Kirk also didn't totally understand why his own cock was thrusting hard against his levis, even though his loved one was kneeling at his feet.

Johnny began to lap Kirk's levi-clad leg as he watched the fucking in the firelight. He felt the tense muscles of his boss and rescuer, and only knew that he wished to serve him whatever his demands might be. The horses stood stock still, braced and trained to maintain tension on the rope regardless of the circumstances.

Juan fucked rhythmically, noting the ecstatic expression of his slave. With one hand he gripped the tense cock and balls of his slave and twisted viciously as he fucked, bringing a gasp to Cal's face but adding to his excitement and pleasure.

"Take it, you cocksuckin' slave," he gritted. "Take my fuckin' prick like a man! Gonna twist your balls off -" He thrust heavily with increasing speed, slamming into his slave swinging on the creaking ropes.

Cal began to moan and struggle, his voice raising to a highpitched wail. Without warning, he spurted white cum in a high arc, coating his belly and his master's hand, and continued jetting gism with each throb of his twisted cock. This brought Juan to climax and he groaned loudly as he filled his slave's ass with his own juice, his prick buried to the hilt. Johnny gripped his man tightly as they watched the frantic display of love and mastery and surrender.

Kirk was stunned by the intensity of the sex but even more shocked by Juan's final move. He bent forward and took his slave in his arms, pulling his close, and kissed him long and hard, his slave's legs wrapped around him.

Kirk looked down at Johnny who was looking up with such yearning, such love in his eyes, that it was like looking into his soul. And when Johnny moved to open Kirk's fly and extract the stiff cock moist with precum, it all fell into place. Johnny took him in to the hilt in one swoop, needing that cock deep in his body, and Kirk trembled with the sudden relief of his long frustration. The heat of that beloved mouth, the welcoming of his huge cock into the cowboy's throat, made him forget Juan and Cal and the weeks of agony and uncertainty that had plagued him.

Without breaking the connection, he slid to the ground and lay beside the Indian, taking the long, bronze cock in his mouth as he had wanted to do for so long. He gripped the young, firm buttocks in both calloused hands and pulled him close, forcing the entire prick down his throat with hunger born of desire and demand. Both felt the need to express love and to accept love, man to man, no holds barred, sucking and being sucked, hot, hot pricks throbbing and thrusting!

They came quickly and together, filling each other with the sweet essence of their love, ignoring Juan and Cal who had come to stand near, their arms around each other. Spurt after spurt of rich cream flooded and soothed their parched throats, each drop a promise and commitment to each other. They had found each other at last.


THE END

# MAN OF NATOMA

The after-work crowd was drifting into Ambush-In-Exile, a different sort of South of Market bar where anything went and usually did. Some were still in work clothes or the tailored shirts and pressed trousers of the daily uniform, thirsty for the first frosty beer of the day and a little conversation with buddies before taking on dinner and the evening's activities. Rory leaned against the bar, his beer half gone, waving to friends as they ducked in the door. There was the usual general feeling of "free at last, where's the party tonight?"

Charlie clapped him on the shoulder and settled on the bar stool next to Rory. "How ya' doing, buddy?"

"Not bad for a Monday," Rory grinned back. "Maybe because I had such a good weekend."

"Oh, yeah? You finally find somebody to lay your ass the way you like it?"

Rory tried to knee him not too gently in the groin but struck his knee on the bar stool instead.

"What d'ya mean, finally? I make out OK, just not as often as I would like - but who does?"

Charlie sighed in concert. "Yeah, I guess so. I really had my ashes hauled yesterday myself, like they haven't been hauled for a while! Thought maybe he'd show up here again tonight..." He looked around hopefully.

Rory kept one eye on the door but looked dreamy. "Me, too. I met this big guy with a beard with a touch of gray, just like I like 'em - a real man - not many like him around..."

Charlie looked at Rory suspiciously. "Big guy with a beard - on a Harley - always wore leather gloves?"

Rory stared back, his attention caught. "Yeah - had a place on Natoma - you know him?"

"Sounds like the guy I met here Sunday afternoon,"

Charlie responded with a far off look in his eye. Again he looked around the filling bar, taking a swig from his bottle, but didn't see that special man he was looking for.

"Oh, come off it - he wouldn't have gone for you, you're too slim and, uh, preppy for this guy."

Charlie gave him a superior, haughty look. "Oh yeah? He said he liked 'em slim and loving, like me, see? Not every master likes a hairy chest, ya know."

"Can't be the same guy. He really dug muscles and mayhem. We wrestled on his leather-covered bed before I finally gave in. Big, rough fucker!"

Charlie was still suspicious. "Oh, yeah? The leather bed fits, too. Tell me more."

"Well," Rory began, "the joint was crowded Saturday night, of course, and even smokier than usual, but I couldn't help noticing steely gray eyes cutting into me from around the post over there. And when he came over toward me, slow and deliberate-like, he never took his eyes off mine. Without a word he gripped one of my tits and twisted it with a gloved paw, a little snarl on his face. I tried not to flinch, but his eyes seemed more threatening than his hand, if you know what I mean. Full leather, jacket, pants, boots, and cap with a brass cock and balls dangling on one side. I just -"

"Who's got a brass cock and balls?" Jack joined the conversation late.

Rory and Charlie greeted their friend with grins. "Rory's just telling me about this stud he met the other night. He sounds familiar, but there's something a little odd - well, go on, what then?"

"Well, I just stared back at him and took another swig of beer. His eyes took a sweep of me and returned to mine. 'You're just about out of beer,' he said. 'Let's have another at my place.' Hell, I haven't heard that direct approach for a long time, especially from a bearded giant with a packed crotch. So before I knew it I was on the

Harley and roarin' off to Natoma."

"Beard? And a Harley? Did the Harley have a lambda sign on the sissy bar?" Jack asked.

"Yeah!" Rory and Charlie said in the same breath. The three looked at each other questioningly. "You, too?" Charlie asked Jack.

"Yeah, I met a guy here just like that last night - tall and husky - solid man's ass - with a Harley..."

"You guys make me sick - do you want to hear the story or not?" Rory growled.

"Sure - sure we do," Charlie and Jack chorused.

"Anyway, he lives in a walk-up apartment on Natoma, but I didn't get to see much of it. He took me into the bedroom and ordered me to undress while he got the beers. Of course I wasn't about to just take orders like that, so I just took my shirt off. When he returned with the beer he acted pretty mad that I hadn't gone all the way, but I just took a swallow of beer and smiled. He was still in full leather, of course."

Rory stopped, apparently reliving the moment, but Charlie and Jack were impatient. "Come on, come on, what then?" Jack asked. Charlie shook his head uncertainly again.

"Well," Rory resumed, "this time he grabbed both my tits and pulled me close. 'So ya want to play rough?' he kind of snarled, and before long we were wrestling on the bed, he's tryin' to get me down and I'm tryin' to keep on top, but he was so fuckin' big and strong that I didn't have a prayer. Pretty soon he had my head locked between his knees and was sittin' on my chest. I guess he didn't know that is my favorite position anyway."

"Only stud in the place who doesn't," Charlie murmured softly. Again he evaded Rory's knee and ignored the insulted look on his buddy's face. "So go ahead, what then?"

"While he is sitting on my chest he took off his leather

jacket and T-shirt, showing off that wide expanse of muscle and chest hair that I just knew was under those clothes. I squirmed around, still fighting a little, but he knew he had me. And especially when he opened his fly and slowly pulled out that monster meat that matched everything else, big and hairy, thick and hard - then I stopped fighting." Again he stopped but continued when his friends promised rather extensive destruction of his anatomy if he didn't.

"He let me get a good look at what was in store for me, slapping my face with it a few times, and then swung around, still sitting on my chest. He got my pants off and gripped my cock and balls in an iron, leather fist that really got my attention, I'll tell ya. Then he swung around again and fed his to me, all ten inches or so, shovin' it down my throat while he was twisting my equipment behind his back. Man, I haven't been face-fucked like that in months - years, maybe. What a stud! When he got close he would pull back and play a little, rubbing that slick cock around my face and jackin' my dick, and then shove back in, clear to the balls.

"I couldn't take too much of that, and I guess he knew it. I started to groan and moan and he really began to pump. My throat was gettin' raw with all that prick shoved down it, but that didn't stop me from shootin' my wad all over his gloved hand. Right about then he filled me full of the sweetest cream this side of heaven, so much that I couldn't swallow it as fast as it came."

"Jeez," Jack breathed, but Charlie just continued to stare.

"I think you dreamed that, Rory - that's not his style at all!"

"Huh? What d'ya mean?"

"Well," Charlie began after stocking up on a fresh one, "it happened here Sunday afternoon. We were all just hangin' out, ya know, shootin' the shit without much goin'

68

on, when this big dude shoulders through the door and everybody stops talkin' just to look. Full leather, tall with a gray-streaked beard, and this little brass cock and balls danglin' from his cap. He got a beer and looked around, and pretty soon he comes saunterin' over to me, a friendly smile on his face, and just stands there for a minute. Then he put one hand up and gently stroked my chin with a big, gloved hand. I hadn't shaved that morning, so it was kind of rough."

"Hell," snorted Jack, "it takes you two days to grow enough beard to even see - don't give us that 'rough' stuff."

"He stroked your chin - gently?" queried Rory.

"Yeah. I was really digging those thick, muscled legs in the leather pants and the long bulge on the left side, but he asked my name and I looked into those clear, gray eyes and almost forgot everything else. He didn't give his name, but bent down and kissed me like I was the most precious thing in the world, but also kind of possessive, ya know? That beard felt real nice...

"Anyway, before long he had me on this Harley and off to Natoma. He laid me out on this leather bed and slowly undressed me, kissing and licking every inch of skin as he uncovered it, concentrating on my tits for a while, and then my belly button, and when he took my pants off I was really hot to trot. I was hopin' he would undress, but he didn't seem to be in any hurry for that. He kind of nibbled around my cock and balls and then lifted my legs up on his shoulders. By this time I was groaning and twisting, ready for just about anything from that sweet, gentle, loving..."

"Sweet? Gentle?" asked Rory unbelievingly.

"Ignore him," Jack instructed. "What happened then?"

"His tongue felt so fuckin' good on my asshole, especially with that beard around it, that I began to beg for it. He must have managed to get his out while he was rimmin' me, 'cause it just seemed like a minor transition from his tongue to his big cock entering me. He held my legs up and shoved all the way in very slowly, and I was soon full of more cock than I've had in many a moon. He started rockin' back and forth, pulling out and shoving in, all the while smilin' down at me with those gentle gray eyes until I was almost hypnotized. I wrapped my legs around his leather shoulders and rocked with the rhythm. My dick was ridin' up his belly and gettin' pretty hot to go. And then I felt him stiffen and that big prick jerkin' inside, and he almost laughed as he shot his big load deep inside. He grabbed my dick in a gloved hand and I shot all over it, just from the love and joy I felt at that moment. It was really nice."

Rory and Jack stared to Charlie in his reverie for a moment, and then all three gulped some more brew.

"Can't be the same guy," Rory muttered.

"Can't be the one I met," Jack agreed. "He was big and broad shouldered and all that, but he came on to me last night as if he was really hungry for a man. I was standin' over there by the juke box in chaps and leather vest, and he cruised me from the bar for a long time before he got up the guts to come over. I just looked him up and down for a minute, and he dropped to his knees, his cheek rubbing my leg for a while, and then looked up at me. When I didn't back away he kissed my crotch and asked if he could service me.

"He was a good six inches taller, but I thought, oh, well, what the hell, 'would be interesting to see what his scene is. I told him to order a cab, but he begged to take me to his place on his bike. Mine's still in the garage, ya know. On the way I started to get hard from his ass rubbing against me on the seat, and he could feel it. Kept backing into it like he was really hard up."

Four eyes glanced at his crotch, familiar with what grew there, but that was before they had become buddies...

"He didn't turn the lights on except a dim one in the bedroom, and brought a couple of beers. He immediately crouched at my feet and began to lick my boots, the best sign of a good slave, and I sipped my beer as he got me warmed up. By the time he worked his way up to my crotch I was ready, and had him undress me slowly as I like. He really moaned when he saw my dick, and I had to push him away at first. I told him to undress, and I liked that broad chest covered with hair on good pecs. But it was his ass that really turned me on - a real man's ass with a hairy cleft just made for a Master's prick. There was a can of Crisco by the bed, and as he slowly lowered his pants I greased up. He was still bent over, pushing down the leathers when I rammed him, all the way to the balls, and he really dug it. He braced himself on the edge of the bed and I gave it to him with both barrels, hard and fast, hot humpin', I can tell you.

"I could see his hand workin' on his dick while all this was goin' on, but I didn't care. His ass was tight and hot, and I pulled his hips to me while I fucked, gettin' hotter by the minute. I couldn't hold back very long, and pretty soon shot my fuckin' load into his gut. I'm pretty sure he shot all over the leather bed at the same time, 'cause he sort of sagged forward and groaned so I had to move forward to give him the last few jets."

"Jeez," Charlie mumbled, adjusting the enlarged bulge in his pants.

"You really fucked him?" Rory mused uncertainly.

"Yeah. He just lay there when I finished, so I finished my beer and left. Wouldn't mind a repeat, though. Thought he might be in here tonight," Jack said quietly.

"I wouldn't, either," Charlie echoed. "Me, too," Rory agreed.

A few minutes of silence passed as they drained down their brews, each mind following its own track.

"How about-" "What if we-" "Maybe we should-" they all started at the same time.

"Are you guys thinkin' what I'm thinkin'?" Jack began again. "Like go over there and give him a real three-way proposition?"

"He can't be all things to all men," Rory answered. "He was a top with me, but then I like tops and like to be face-fucked. With you he was a bottom, and with Charlie he was a lover. Nobody can be all those things. We got to settle this, once and for all!"

They stared at each other for a moment, and then with one accord slammed down their empty bottles on the bar and trooped out, straight to Natoma Street.

The outside door was open as before, and they clumped up the stairs to the familiar door. They knocked several times but there was no answer. Then an old lady appeared at the foot of the stairs, asking what they wanted.

"We want to talk to the guy who lives here. Do you know where he is?" Jack inquired politely.

"Nobody lives there - haven't had anybody in that apartment for over a month," was the firm reply. "Are you interested in renting it?"

The three guys looked at each other in amazement. Rory was the first to recover.

"Uh, yeah, we'd like to look it over, since it's vacant," he said, and the others nodded. So the old lady grunted her way up the stairs, opened the door, and they crowded in.

There was no furniture of any kind in the large living room they entered. None of them knew much about the apartment except for the bedroom, and they headed for it immediately. It was also empty.

The three friends stared at each other and at the empty room, visualizing again the massive, bearded leather man who had fulfilled their favorite fantasies.

72

The old lady was impatient. "One of you interested in renting it? Only one bedroom, ya know. I could make a good deal for a nice, quiet working man."

Again the men looked around the room, each busy with his own thoughts, but then each shook his head. The old lady sighed and led the way out.

Rory was the last to leave. His toe contacted a small object and he bent to pick it up as the others filed out. It was a small pin, a brass cock and balls.

THE END

A hard man is good to find.
Sometimes it's better not to
ask too many questions.

# ON THE ROAD

Cory yawned hugely, his protruding thumb drooping with fatigue. How long had he been on this fuckin' highway with his thumb out, hoping for that hitch to somewhere, anywhere out of this desert small town rat race? Twelve, fourteen hours? In the blinding sun, inhaling the blacktop fumes and exhausts of gas guzzlers burning their way to palm tree-shaded paradises west.

He had had to leave. He had thought about it for weeks, the grinding boredom of work in the gas station in his small, isolated Arizona town, his quarrelsome parents hemmed in by geography and ignorance, the guys and girls sopping up beer in the rundown roadside bar that passed for entertainment but more often led to fistfights because there was nothing much else to do. California - that's where the action is, he thought.

He hadn't slept at all last night, thinking of taking the plunge. And then, before dawn, he had thrown some clothes into his tattered canvas bag and left - just left it all behind, looking for - something, anything, and anywhere but "home".

A ponderous Cadillac with four old geezers in it swished by without a glance at the bronzed blond with his thumb out. Why should they care, after all? They were probably headed for a cool pool in Palm Springs, or some such. Cory used his sodden handkerchief to sop up the sweat running down his bare chest. At least he had had his hair cut short last week, so that wasn't falling into his face. His crotch was dripping, too, and the hot sun kept his cock on the verge of erection. He had an impulse to take it out and beat off, all alone in the desert, but what the hell - beating off alone was one of the things he was hoping to get away from!

A dark shape crept into view over the distant ridge

75

line. As it drew closer, Cory could see it was a large van, painted black and with no side windows. The darkness was only relieved by a gray stripe that splashed its side. It braked to a stop at his feet. At last, a ride!

Cory didn't even look at the driver until he was inside, the air conditioning a welcome relief from the blistering heat. Then his eyes met piercing black ones, drilling him from under a floppy black hat of nondescript vintage. A mustache and beard with sprinklings of gray framed a strong jaw. He wore a leather vest over a bare chest that was almost black from the sun and liberally decorated with curly dark hair, especially around prominent pectorals. Faded jeans covered his legs, but his feet were bare.

"Where ya headed?" a deep voice issued from curving lips, the eyes appraising him openly.

"You're heading west, right? That's where I'm heading," Cory answered honestly, noticing the bulging arm muscles and obvious strength in the broad hands resting quietly on the steering wheel. Again those eyes drilled into him, seeming to read him like an open book.

The driver slipped into gear and back onto the highway, accelerating rapidly toward the setting sun.

"Name's Buck."

"Mine's Cory."

Buck nodded, his eyes on the road. "Running away?"

Cory blushed. The question sounded childish, like a kid with a beef against his mother or something.

"In a way," he answered, his eyes straight ahead.

"Looking for something?"

Cory hesitated a moment. Maybe this guy was reading him too well. "Yeah, guess so."

There were several moments of silence. "Hungry?" Buck asked in a kinder tone.

"As a matter of fact - "

"There's a sandwich in that bag and a beer in the

cooler behind your seat."

Cory opened the brown bag next to him and extracted a thick meat sandwich that made his stomach growl. He looked behind the seat and found the cooler and snagged a can from its icy contents. He noticed the darkness of the open, empty van that had no windows but was fitted with some sort of metal bars. Even the floor was covered with thick, black carpeting. At that moment only the food and drink interested him.

"Sure it's OK?" he asked politely, not wanting to take the guy's food without at least an inquiry.

"Sure," Buck answered, smiling for the first time. "Eat up."

Cory lost no time in downing the sliced beef and washing it down with cool beer, his first food of the day. The van purred smoothly down the deserted highway. The driver was silent, and soon Cory's lids began to grow heavy from the hypnotic sound and the lack of sleep. For some reason he felt very comfortable with this stranger droning along the deserted highway in the gathering gloom. Soon he was nodding drowsily and Buck noticed.

"Why don't you stretch out in the back? The carpet's thick and you can catch up on your zzz's," he suggested.

Offering no objection, Cory twisted out of the bucket seat and stretched out on the floor of the dark van, in a deep sleep almost as soon as he touched down.

It must have been an hour or two later that he suddenly awoke. It was totally dark outside, but there were candles lit in the van that was now stationary, apparently some distance off the road as judged by the distant traffic sounds from the highway. But what had disturbed his sleep was his body being moved, his leg stretched to the far side of the van. And then he realized that one arm and one leg were manacled to a steel bar running down the length of the van, and Buck, entirely naked except for his battered hat, was strapping his other leg to a bar on the other side, spreading him wide and immobilized. He also realized for the first time that he was also entirely naked!

"What the fuck -" he began, but Buck only grunted, seizing his free arm and wrestling it to the mat with ease, securely enclosing it in a leather manacle and snapping it to the bar. Cory was spread-eagled, and his struggles against the restraints were obviously useless. Buck looked down at him with satisfaction.

"You were sleeping really hard, man. Sorry to disturb you - " - his smile belied his regret - "but it's time you learned a few facts of life," he said grimly, his broad hands on his hips, his thick, hairy legs spread like a stallion. In the dim, flickering light, Cory could see a thick cock beginning to rise from its dark bush.

"Let me go!" Cory pleaded. "What the fuck are you doing?" He was suddenly quivering, unable to move, his muscles stretched tightly, as the forbidding monster towered over him. What had he got himself into?

Buck didn't answer but began to stroke his prick to full staff, his eyes boring into his victim's. The throbbing prick took on the aspects of a huge club, threatening him with mayhem of unknown character. It was only then that he realized that his own cock was growing tall, throbbing between his legs and jerking with each heart beat as the towering, scowling master draw closer to him. As if to continue the analogy, the man's now rigid cock also resembled a horse's in length and thickness.

When Buck suddenly dropped to his knees between Cory's legs, he thought the end was at hand. But instead of a crushing blow to his throbbing genitals, it was a warm, moist mouth that engulfed his cock, quickly taking the entire organ into its depths. Cory groaned from the sudden heat and delicious shock, made more intense as the lips drew back to the head, sucking it hard, before taking it all again to the balls.

"Christ!" he moaned. It would almost have been better to counter a vicious attack than that excruciating pleasure that suffused his body stretched taut by the leather straps. He struggled and twisted, but realized that he was thrusting toward his torturer and that avid mouth rather than trying for the impossible escape. Buck took him into his throat, apparently enjoying the throbbing fullness filling him with maleness.

"Please -" Cory begged, but he was not sure what he wanted at that moment. His cock lurched strongly and his balls churned hotly, and suddenly release was his greatest need. No longer were his bonds the prime concern, but the demands of his body were focused in his cock.

The hot lips and tongue pulled and pumped, each movement curling his toes and bringing his balls close to explosion. Quivering, Cory moaned and wished for release while at the same time hoping it would continue.

Apparently sensing some degree of surrender, Buck drew back, allowing the cock to jerk damply in the air. Then he moved forward, straddling the torso of his trembling victim. Slowly he lowered himself, taking the dripping prick into his ass as Cory whimpered in fear and lust. At first it was tight, his weight pressing on the stiff cock and bending it slightly. But then he opened up and Cory entered the hot ass as Buck eased himself lower. Cory tried to move away, but it was no use. Buck held his cock in place and soon he was impaled on the unwilling prick.

As the new sensation flooded his senses, the hot clutching tightness gripping him despite his vain attempts to free himself, Cory moaned again. He could feel the man's heavy cock resting on his belly, the bulbous head damp with precum. His own cock was almost gobbled up by the hungry asshole, swallowing him and adding new torture to his flaming frustrations.

"There ya go, man, right up my ass," Buck breathed as he stared at the blond struggling in his fetters. "Hot dick up a hot ass."

"Ugh!" Cory thrust upward, suddenly needing that extra inch of contact, needing to be consumed by that flaming cauldron that set his own fires flaring. "Oh, shit, take it all," he heard himself begging, mashing his balls painfully against his attacker.

Buck's smile was fleeting and menacing as he began to rotate around the pole filling him, knowing all the tricks for bringing a fresh victim figuratively to his knees. Cory felt his cock was being sucked into a heated trap, and he knew that soon he would lose his cum to the irresistible demands of this man so much his master. His helplessness, his inability to move in any significant way, added to the intensity; he had no control at all. Buck had no mercy - his ass moved in circles and up and down as he watched the strain increase on his victim's face.

"Ugh - ugh - " Cory groaned through clenched teeth, powerless to resist the castrating force that had transformed his body into an object with only one goal, that of firing his cum with a velocity that might blow his head off. He must - he had to cum - he had to -

He screamed with the intensity of his orgasm, the candlelights dancing in his tormented brain, the hot ass clenching and stroking each spurt from his balls drawn up tight for maximum explosion. Buck squirmed and twisted, drawing out every bit of juice his slave could muster, watching Cory struggle to resist and losing the battle. Only when the struggles stopped and the muscles suddenly collapsed did Buck settle down, feeling the last feeble twitches deep in his ass. The black eyes bored into Cory's from under the shapeless hat.

Buck sat stroking his stiff cock slowly as he watched recovery slowly taking place. Finally Cory's eyes opened, his pupils wide, not sure he was still in one piece. When he was able to focus on Buck with his intense and threatening stare, he shuddered for what else might be in store although grateful for what had been the most devastating orgasm he had ever experienced. Unable to resist, he had been drained of his manhood for the pleasure of this strange man in his secret lair.

Buck rose, allowing the softening cock to escape from its prison, but he wasn't finished. Reaching behind him he snagged a long steel rod; he placed it across Cory's ankles and snapped the manacles to rings in its ends. Cory's feet were freed from the van but still spread widely by the new rod. Buck lifted the feet high and towards his victim's head so his knees were somewhat bent. He fastened the spreading rod to hooks in the van roof, bringing Cory's ass up for his close inspection.

"No, not that, please -" Cory pleaded, realizing what could happen to him, what that huge cock could do to him. He struggled against his bonds but it was useless. His shoulders were still on the floor and the blood rushed to his head. Buck merely grunted and spread the firm buns with his strong thumbs.

"That virgin ass needs some attention," he said, tracing the outlines of the tiny rosette with his fingers. Cory lurched up and down, since that movement was the only one possible to him, but he could not evade the probing assault. His actions seemed to inflame his tormenter even more.

Kneeling and spreading him wide, Buck placed his lips squarely on the tossing asshole. His tongue circled the dark opening but then began to enter and probe the moving target, riding him like a bucking horse. He could feel the sphincter tighten and then begin to relax, and gradually the struggles lessened as his tongue soothed and tantalized. Cory gasped; even as he struggled against the insistent demands, he was becoming aware of a totally new sensation, a spreading warmth radiating from his ass on which his tormenter was feeding.

"Oh, Christ, don't -" Cory began, but then realized that he was struggling, not to escape, but to force more and more of that raping tongue into his ass, needing the exquisite torment in some mysterious way even though his brain tried to resist it. He could feel the invasion deeper with each thrust of the stiffened tongue and hoped it would never stop.

Buck stopped; it was time for the main event. He rose and spread some saliva on his rearing cock, his gaze fixed on the dripping asshole of his victim.

"No, please -" Cory began but then broke off. He wasn't really sure he wanted Buck to stop.

He felt the broad cockhead against his asshole. It was hot and fleshy, hard but spongy. It entered, slowly and deliberately. The huge prick plowed its way inward. He was being stretched wide and painfully, the huge cock insisting on its rights, but Cory's struggles ceased as the invasion proceeded. It seemed right, somehow, that he be conquered by that rigid, living flesh and the man who bore it. He sagged into his bonds as his body was filled, slowly but inexorably, the pain converted to a general feeling of giddy acceptance, of being conquered by a rightful master in the most appropriate way conceivable.

"That's it, take my dick, man," Buck urged softly, feeling the tension leave the trussed body. He could see the little smile forming around Cory's lips and the eyes close for the moment to savor the experience. "Take it all the way. You need it."

The fullness was becoming unbelievable. Further and further the huge prick pressed, and Cory gasped with the enormity while at the same time wanting more. The pain was still there but was being replaced by a feeling of satiation, of fulfillment. When he felt the hairy balls against his ass he knew he had it all, and he was pleased.

His eyes opened to Buck's taut body pressed hard

against him. The bronze muscles rippled as Buck began to move, first in small circles, bringing a wider smile to Cory's lips, and then with short thrusts that emphasized his mastery. Cory watched in fascination and growing enjoyment as Buck strained against him, knowing that he was taking this man to the hilt and bringing his juices toward the surface. He could see the ecstatic excitement replacing the scowl on his master's face, and understood the extreme pleasure his ass was bringing to his conqueror.

"Go ahead, fuck me," he said deliberately, knowing he could take it - knowing that he wanted it. His own cock was hard and throbbing again.

Buck's eyes glittered and he began to fuck, long, slow strokes, watching the expression on his victim's face. He resolved to wipe away some of that tranquility.

He began to thrust heavily, deeply, entering further than ever before. Each thrust was rigidly penetrating, the hot, young ass inviting him to supreme efforts. He was rewarded by a growing subtle expression of fear and uncertainty on Cory's face as he fucked him with increasing force. The smile was still fixed, but there was an element of poorly understood threat that Buck needed. The young cock bobbed rigidly, unattended.

Buck gripped Cory's balls and pulled downward, gently at first and then more forcefully as he continued to fuck. Cory's expression did not change. Even as Buck twisted the tortured orbs, Cory tried to show no fear.

"Fuck me," he repeated quietly, but the increasing violence gave him some misgivings. The huge cock deep in his bowels brought a satisfaction that he had never experienced before, but even more potent was the knowledge that he was able to take it all without screaming in terror. Each thrust became stronger, conquering and encompassing everything that had ever happened before. The pressure on his balls added to his soaring spirits, and he felt his own juices beginning to boil.

"Man, I'm goin' to fill you up! Goin' to fill you full of my fuck-cream right up your ass!"

"Yes, yes - " Cory gasped, ready for the culmination of this violent coupling, needing the climax from this man who filled him with virility, who controlled him so completely. It was important to be filled with the hot life force of this man who controlled him. He was the willing receptacle for his passions.

"Ugh - yeah - take it!" Buck shouted, thrusting hard and deep, spurting hotly as he gave up his very essence. Again he thrust, and this time was rewarded with the first spurt from the ignored cock of his victim, streaming whitely in the air and splattering them both.

Cory also screamed, the intensity of the mutual orgasm shattering his dream-state with ecstasy that swept away all semblance of reason. Together they vented their lust in shared violence in that black van in the middle of the desert.

As their climaxes passed they stared at each other, shaken with the intensity of their experience.

Buck finally moved back, his cock slipping free. With shaking hands he lowered Cory's legs and removed the manacles. He knelt by his side and unstrapped his wrists. Cory did not move from his bondage position but merely looked up at his master with wonder and contentment. It was right, somehow, to be laid out as a victim to this man at this place.

Buck spread himself over him, lowering himself gently, and gathered him into his arms. They kissed, the dark beard bristling against the smooth, blond face as their lips mashed together and their tongues spoke silently to each other.

Cory, his arms free at last, clasped Buck to his chest. There was serenity now, a confidence that he knew who he was and where he was going. The muscular body in his arms felt natural and right, and for the first time that he could remember he was rid of confusion and doubt.

Vaguely he realized that what he had sought was this, the masculine body in his arms, the sharing of life with one who understood him, could guide him and even punish him if needed; a man who would mold him to be the best he could be.

He was, finally, free.


THE END

Sometimes freedom means being
tied to a post - as long as it's
the right post and in far enough.

# BRIDGING THE GAP

I shuddered deliciously as my Master emerged from the spare bedroom. He had chosen to wear a black leather executioner's mask over his handsome face, but I could see the blue eyes flashing imperiously through the slits. His thin lips held the hint of a snarl over the short full beard streaked with gray, the same mixture of black and gray that matted his broad, naked chest.

The black leather chaps hugged his rugged legs tightly; the leather creaked tantalizingly as he stalked slowly toward me. Under the chaps he had cupped his thick cock and heavy, hairy balls into a black leather jockstrap that already bulged menacingly. If he allowed me, it would be my pleasure to bring that glorious instrument of manhood to full staff and drain those perfectly-matched balls of some of their burden of life-giving sperm. If he allowed me.

He stood over me for a moment as I knelt naked on the floor in deserved humility, looking up at my paragon, my Master-prince who sometimes allowed me to serve him. About once a week, when he could leave his wife and children, Arthur made a curt call to me, a call I yearned for, suffering when it did not come, responding frantically when it did. "I'll be there around eight." "Yes, Sir."

I salivated as my eyes traveled up his massive leather legs, his flat hairy belly, his nipples hiding in their hairy nests, to the bright blue glints piercing the torturers hood. His work-worn hands rested challengingly on his slim hips. Those rough hands, thickened from swinging a hammer and handling rough lumber, could bring stinging welts to my tender skin when it suited my Master.

I knew he was a carpenter, a construction foreman, and his eldest son worked with him as an apprentice. I had met the son once at work - a clean-shaven version of his father but without the domineering swagger. Arthur had complete control over his crew, almost as complete as his control over me at that moment.

My gaze was drawn irresistibly to the leather-encased trio of jewels thrusting in concealment from their hairy adornment. I licked my lips and my mouth sagged open with anticipation. The jockstrap pouch seemed to stretch more under my longing gaze.

Seeming satisfied with my obvious, pleading desire, he turned to show his virile, rounded ass and broad back with their strapping muscles outlined magnificently in the soft, low light. The saliva flowed copiously as I tasted in memory the slightly salty skin and the aphrodisiacal musk of his ass crack which I might sample again. If he allowed me. The leather straps of the jockstrap made no dent in the hard buttocks outlined roundly by the chaps. For the first time I noticed the cat-o'-nine-tails, the thongs wrapped around the studded handle, hanging by a hook from one leather-clad hip.

He moved backward slowly, straddling me. My eyes were fixed on the shadowy crack with its crisp hair centering on the object of my desire, and as he moved over me I leaned backward until I was flat, spread-eagled as was fitting. I was aware that my cock, encircled by its studded leather strap (the only covering he allowed me), was thudding stiffly aloft, but it was of no consequence. I gazed upward, swallowing convulsively, the shadows partially concealing his asshole and the globular testicles nearly escaping from their leather casing. I needed him badly. If he allowed me.

Slowly his knees bent, the leather creaking musically. Slowly, so slowly, his ass drew nearer to my face until I could feel the heat generated from his fragrant crotch. The balls rolled gently, his position exposing more of their hairy shapes to my adoring eyes. And then I could see clearly the puckered lips of his beckoning asshole, but I knew I was not allowed to move toward him, much as I wished to. My fingers scrabbled in the carpeting, aching to touch, desperate to pull his leather legs down and press those pink lips to mine, to kiss my Master in the only proper way.

Just when I thought I might get my wish, he rose up slowly, tearing the possibility from my grasp. As he rose he freed the cat and I could tell he was separating the thongs for their intended work. I stiffened involuntarily, and knew that my cock was throbbing even stronger, tossing its head impatiently.

The first slash was gentle, a stinging kiss of the knotted tips of the thongs to the head of my cock. It lurched, needing more. The second slash was more deliberate, the thongs scoring the length of my cock and imparting even more rigidity, my need growing more urgent. The third blow was deliciously vicious, striping the already florid prick in streaks of vermilion. I jerked and groaned, and he grunted in satisfaction. I knew there was a twisted smile on his face although he was still turned away. As his arm rose and fell again and again, enforcing his leather will on my sacrificial body, the muscles in his back bunched and tightened as they must every day as he labored in construction.

I grasped his leather-encased ankles, supportive as trees, and I imagined myself tied between two redwoods in the middle of a forest, the blows raining down on my slumping frame for my Master's amusement. I spread my legs wider to conform to that image, and the whip lashed my exposed balls in its next trajectory. Again I jerked, moaning with the sudden, dull pain, and he breathed, "Yeahhh." I could see that his cock was so rigid it was stretching the soft pouch of the jockstrap outward, fully exposing his hairy balls. With each blow my balls contracted, preparing to pump out their engorged contents if my Master wished.

"Raise your knees and spread 'em, slave," he growled, his first command. Until then my actions had been reflexive, but I knew what he wanted. I obeyed quickly, and the next blow included my clenching asshole. My entire crotch was being set afire by the kiss of the leather, my ass punished by the knotted ends of the whip for desiring him and my balls stroked fiercely for threatening to disgorge; my cock throbbed rigidly as the thongs wound around it in smarting embrace. My arms ached from my own fierce grip of the leather trunks straddling me.

He suddenly stopped. Either he was becoming tired or bored, I couldn't determine which. He turned around to face me, confirming that twisted smile I had envisioned on his face. He held the studded whip handle casually in one hand and in the other hand the narrow thongs, drooping in an innocent arc. I looked into his eyes and knew I had satisfied him - so far. My heart sang.

Again, slowly, very slowly, he lowered himself toward my face. My mouth gaped for him but it was not to be. Instead he sat on my chest, his knees clamping my head between them in a leather vice. The aroma of his leather and his ass and his balls and his cock - him! - enveloped me and sent new messages of longing to my aching groin. His prick filled the leather pouch and protruded nearly to my mouth. His warm balls nestled onto my chest, their hairs mingling obscenely with mine.

"You're hungry, aren't you, kid," he stated matter-of-factly.

I nodded mutely, gulping again even though my mouth was dry. I looked from the leather-covered projection to his eyes and back again, mutely begging for him, but instead he filled my vacant mouth with the studded whip handle, forcing my lips open widely, grinding the steel studs against my teeth. I sucked it greedily as best I could, grateful for at least a taste of him, something that belonged to him. The leather still bore the warmth and aroma of his hands.

"Fucking cocksucker," he grunted, his lips curving. Our eyes locked as he twisted and thrust the studded dildo into my mouth. From the black mask of the executioner those blue lasers burned into my brain and turned my mouth into a mere receptacle, hypnotically accepting whatever he wished to present.

"Yes, I"m a cocksucker!" I signalled mutely. "I'm your cocksucker - if you'll have me! I'll eat out your ass, or I'll drink your piss, or I'll be the whipping boy for all your daily frustrations, as long as it is you! My Master..." But he knew all that; his presumption was global. I could feel him begin to tremble slightly. I hoped it meant what I thought it meant...

He removed the whip handle and twisted his body around. He wrapped the thongs of the whip around my cock, overlapping the thongs in such a way that it pulled tightly as he yanked. The thongs made sensuous grooves in the tender skin, a different but similar kiss to those made earlier as they had whistled through the air. Then, turning back to me and still holding the whip handle, he moved forward to press his stiff, leather-clad prick into my mouth.

It was warm, almost hot, from all the blood dammed up in that thick stalk. The taste of leather and a trace of cum from previous orgasms was ambrosia. His hairy balls nudged my chin, urging me on (as if I needed it). I slurped and sucked, the wet leather conforming to the shape of his prick. Yes, I'm a cocksucker - a leather cocksucker! I screamed silently.

"You're a leather cocksucker, kid," he snarled. He always knew what I was thinking.

He pulled the whip taut, the thongs digging deeper into my cock. I tried to take all of him, the leather filling the corners of my mouth not engorged with his cock. The harder I sucked, the harder he pulled. I could see his mouth tighten, his teeth clench.

"Oh, shit, kid, you're goin' to get it!"

With one hand he scooped out his rigid dick from the leather pouch and - at last! - shoved the naked, throbbing rod down my throat. He gasped and his head swiveled upward as my throat closed around the bulging head sweet with juice and leather. I gobbled in as much as I could as he leaned forward, fucking my face. I was filled with the mantool of my Master, the supreme moment in every slave's life.

I gloried in the moment because I knew it wouldn't last very long. His balls roiled on my chin, and as he pulled out slightly I tasted him again, sweeter than before. He tightened his grip on the tether around my cock, and I arched in an effort to delay the inevitable.

A thrust in, a short withdrawal, and then he groaned loudly as if he regretted the moment. But there was no turning back. The first spurt of juice was explosive - sweet, thick, and potent. With the violence of his orgasm he pulled roughly on the thongs, almost amputating the head of my prick before I shot my own cum wildly over my belly. He continued to gush into my mouth, matched by my own spasms of joy and release that soaked the thongs and spattered up to my chest.

Only after he had emptied his reservoirs did he release me and then leaned forward on his elbows, his cock deeply imbedded in my throat. I couldn't see his face, but I knew the tension was gone. His slave had performed adequately.

He never stayed long after cuming. It was a ritual that I thoroughly cleanse his spent cock with a warm, damp cloth, but it must be done gently because he was exquisitely sensitive. Then he dressed in silence and, nudging my arm with a closed fist, said "I'll call you, kid."

I hoped he would.

The next evening I was thinking about Arthur. It was a warm night, and I was knocking around the house in my cut-off levis. "Kid", he always called me, but I was only about ten years younger than he. On the few occasions he did stay around long enough to talk, he had finally admitted (largely to himself) that he was bisexual. Obviously his family didn't know about this extra side of him; he kept his leathers alongside mine in my closet to maintain secrecy. He truly led a double life.

The doorbell rang and I answered the door. "Artie!" I said, startled. Arthur's son was the last person in the world I expected on my doorstep! There was a motorcycle leaning on its kickstand in my driveway.

Artie was obviously embarrassed, mumbling apologies for dropping in as I helped him off with his leather jacket. I was struck again by the similarities between father and son - the same muscular body structure, the same startlingly blue eyes and aquiline face - but I had never seen his father uncertain of himself as Artie appeared to be that evening. I opened beers for both of us and he sat tensely, looking at me.

Without asking the reason for his visit, I inquired about their latest construction project and that seemed to put him at ease, and then about motorcycles ( he was quite an enthusiast), but we quickly ran out of conversation topics. He sat rather stiffly on the couch and I sprawled across from him in a leather chair, my favorite spot. Eventually he started to open up, but hesitantly.

"I suppose you think its - queer - " - he hesitated on the word, looking quickly at me for my reaction - "coming to you like this, but I know you are a friend of my dad's and - I can't talk about this with him. I figured - you - might understand, or be able to - "

I nodded silently, wondering what I was getting into, and whether Arthur would be annoyed if he knew his son was talking to me like this. I tried to look encouraging.

"My dad's such a - man's man, you know - " I nodded, knowing even better than he - "he wouldn't understand. But I have these dreams - fantasies, I guess you'd call them. And they bother me, and I don't know how to handle them."

I nodded, wondering if I should refer him to a psychiatrist or something. But he went on.

"Especially when I get my leather jacket on and ride around on the bike, I get these thoughts about other guys in leather and - uh, having sex with them." Uh-oh. I guess my face didn't reveal my inner feelings, because he continued.

"Only it's not the usual kind of - queer stuff I read about, sucking each other's cock and things like that. It's more - a lot more - and sometimes my Dad is involved in those dreams - I don't know - "

He broke off, blushing furiously, and I was aware that my cock was beginning to grow. "More - what?" I asked a little breathlessly.

He sighed, as if wishing on one hand that he hadn't started the discussion, but now was determined to see it through.

"Like being stripped down and tied up, or forced by an older guy - that gives me a hardon, just thinking about it. Like you."

Like me? What did he mean - and then I followed his gaze to my crotch where my cock was beginning to push out of the leg of my cut-offs. It was my turn to blush, but I didn't try to hide my excitement. He watched it grow, which didn't help the situation. He was a beautiful man.

"Have you - had any experience like that?" I asked hoarsely. He shook his head. "Are you sure you want it?" He nodded, meeting my eyes for a long moment before dropping his gaze again to my nearly stiff cock protruding from the cut-offs.

I don't think I could have stopped then if I tried, but I had fleeting thoughts of how angry his father, my Master, would be if he found out I had diddled with his son, mixed with an intense desire to do it anyway. After all, the boy needed help, didn't he? Someone had to do it, didn't they? He was pretty miserable as he was.

"Wait here," I said. My first order. I went into the bedroom and returned a few minutes later nude except for a leather jockstrap and chaps, and a stern expression on my face. I brought with me a long, steel bar with manacles attached. His jaw fell and he gulped, dropping his empty beer can on the floor. "Wow," he breathed.

"Come here, kid," I commanded. He stared at me for a moment and then rose quickly to stand in front of me. "Take off those sissy clothes," I snarled, and started by ripping his plaid shirt open, popping a few buttons on the way. In a daze he hastened to comply, but I noticed his repeated glances at my jock which was doing an incomplete job of holding me in. I had barely been able to stuff it all into the pouch in my semi-rigid state.

In a moment he was bare-assed naked, a beautiful specimen so like his father. His ass was even more perfect, and his cock and balls were almost a spitting image. He didn't have all the chest hair his father had, but his prick was hard and throbbing and ready.

"On your knees, kid," I growled, and he immediately knelt before me, looking up with expectant, bright eyes, his gaze traveling over my hairy chest and down to my crotch.

"Don't touch unless I give permission!" I barked, as he reached tentatively toward the leather. He brought his arms rigidly to his sides. He looked up at me startled.

"OK," he assented.

"Yes, Sir! is the proper form of address!" I growled again. His face fell but his eyes grew brighter.

"Yes, Sir!" he answered enthusiastically, sounding more like a Marine recruit than a slave.

I reached down and began to play with his tits. They were virginal, of course, and I had to tease them a bit to bring them up, but soon I was twisting none too gently, watching his face. I could see flashes of pain but they were quickly replaced with smiles.

"What are you smiling about, kid?" I demanded. He sobered quickly, especially when I gave them both a vicious twist.

"Stand up here," I instructed, and he quickly got to his feet, his prick rigidly horizontal. I surveyed the material, turning him this way and that, and finally gave his cock a cuff, sending it slapping against his hairy thigh. That brought a gasp to his lips but did not lessen the stiffness.

"Turn around." His back was ridged with muscles that rippled with the slightest arm movements. His legs were heavily muscled and hairy, but his ass was hairless and taut. "Bend over," I ordered, pushing on his back, and he complied willingly, his upturned ass bringing even more discomfort to my constrained cock. Roughly I caressed those smooth, rounded buns, sensing his trembling, and then pushed him down on my leather-clad knee. I began to spank him, fairly gently at first and then harder and harder, the smacks echoing sharpely.

"Yes, Daddy, yes, Sir!" he groaned. I alternated buns until they both took on a rosy hue. He squirmed against me, the leather chafing his belly, and I could feel his cock jabbing my leg stiffly as he moved. "Yes, Sir, Daddy!" he almost cried but he was loving it, I could tell.

I stopped abruptly and raised him up. His eyes were moist but there was no weakness there. His gaze met mine steadily, and he was as rigid as before. I gripped his cock and balls roughly in one hand and began to twist.

"A little punishment gets you all stiff and excited,

doesn't it, kid," I sneered, knowing exactly how he felt. His thick prick and large, hairy balls felt good in my hand as I twisted them. I watched his face contort briefly, first with the pleasant shock of another man's touch and then the dull pain produced as they were treated to a taste of sadistic manhandling. He tried to maintain an undisturbed demeanor, but it wasn't easy. My pressure increased, going pretty far before his defiance started to crumble. I didn't want to go too far with the kid the first time. That could come later. I released him.

"Lie down on your back on the floor," I snapped, and he obediently complied. By this time I wouldn't have been surprised at some reluctance on his part, but no. I spread his ankles and placed the heavy bar on them, strapping his ankles to it with the leather manacles. His young, heavy balls hugged the base of his cock, and I tied a leather thong tightly around the set. Quickly they turned red from the trapped blood and looked even better.

I saw him strain once to raise his legs, but that was impossible. I straddled his chest and he looked up at me, those blue lights almost caressing the leather clad legs, the tense leather jockstrap, the bare chest, and the stern expression on my face. I had brought the whip with me but decided not to use it, not this time.

"A kid like you is good for only one thing," I snarled at him. "To service a man's crotch."

By his expression I could tell he wasn't really sure what that entailed, and for the first time I saw a trace of concern on that handsome face. Good. Slowly I lowered myself, the leather binding deliciously around my knees, and the closer I got to his face the wider his eyes became. They were fixed on the cock bulge, so I decided to postpone that for the moment. As I grew close I shifted forward so that my asshole was directly over his mouth.

From the quick intake of breath and the sudden shocked expression on his face, I knew that he had never thought of eating a guy's ass before. He focused on that pink pucker and his look of distaste gave me my first real satisfaction. I had finally gotten through to him.

He started to squirm but I moved with him. I gave him a quick slap on one cheek and then clamped his face between my legs.

"Lick out my asshole, kid, your Master likes his asshole clean and you're going to make sure it's clean."

He shot me a look that almost made me relent. Instead I sat down squarely on his mouth. Again he tried to squirm away but I held him fast. I could feel those ruby lips trembling against me, and I waited.

After a moment his tongue snaked out. I knew he was trying to evade direct contact, but I kept him under control. Once more he looked up at me around the near-bursting cock pouch, his eyes full of mixed messages, but then he closed them and began to lap my asshole. He didn't do it well, of course, but he did it.

I didn't prolong it, mostly because I couldn't take the exquisite pleasure very long. My cock was so painful in its leather casing that I had to move on to the next step. I raised up, my ass cool and tingling, and we stared at each other. Then I moved back and surprised him by bending down and kissing him on the mouth. That startled him, too, but he quickly got into that act. That was a trap, I decided, but I had made a point.

"You like leather, don't you, kid? Well how about a leather cock in your mouth - do you like that, too?" I pressed my bulge into his face and after a moment of hesitation he opened his mouth for it. Watching him take me like that brought all my lust to the fore, and I almost came, more from the sight than the feel. I stuffed all the cock and leather I could into his mouth, making him choke on his own spit. I glanced back over my shoulder and, as I expected, his cock was rigid and jerking, not at all turned off by what I was putting him through. It was *piece de resistance* time!

I partially pulled out and managed to snake the leather pouch off without complete withdrawal. As soon as the moist heat of his mouth struck my cock skin I knew I couldn't hold out very long.

He gripped my leather legs, perhaps resisting the inevitable. I took both his hands in mine and stretched his arms over his head, holding them down solidly to the floor in a rape position. There was some resistance at first, the realization of his position clear. Then I felt him relax into the carpeting almost gratefully. With his legs spread and anchored to the heavy steel bar, he was completely immobilized.

There it was, the moment of truth at last. He had a man's cock in his mouth, a hot, throbbing one oozing pre-cum over his tongue, and he couldn't escape. I don't know how many times he had fantasized this moment or whether the reality lived up to the fantasy, but I know it was a high point for me, watching my cock go in and out of that manly mouth, knowing it was his first time. His teeth were a problem, but not much. I knew I couldn't last long enough for any real damage.

"You're a fucking cocksucker, kid," I grated. I am not sure he heard me through the clamor in his brain.

I put it about half way in and stopped. He looked up at me with such happiness, almost akin to worship, that I almost melted. But instead I shoved it in further until he choked and then pulled out most of the way. The scraping teeth only added to my delirium, and I gave him a few more thrusts before the moment was at hand.

"Oh, shit, kid, you're goin' to get it!" I flooded him with hot cum and the top of my head blew off.

Immediately he choked. That's not an easy position to take a load, as we all know. I pulled up for a moment, meanwhile spraying more over his lips, and again filled his mouth. Tears came to his eyes, but he was game. He didn't give up, only gasped for air now and then. A beautiful man.

As my spurts tapered off and my blood pressure came down a few points, I swiveled, pushing my softening cock into his throat. Again he choked but I just shoved it in. I grabbed his throbbing dick and gave it a couple of rough twists. That was enough to start it spurting high and white, thick gobs flying over his belly and chest and covering my hand. His entire body went into convulsive gyrations, his legs thrashing and his belly muscles bending him into arcs of joy. His jaws clamped down on my cock but I didn't care. I had a strong urge to lap up the cream that coated him, but I didn't.

After he quieted I rose and stood over him, milking the last few drops onto his cum-smeared face. I don't think I have ever seen such clarity of expression of joy and relief on anyone's face, before or since.

I untied his cock-ball thong and unstrapped his ankles. I gave him a hand up and pulled him close to me. His hunky body leaned into mine and our moist, softening cocks nuzzled each other. He put his head on my shoulder and we stood there for several minutes until I could feel his heart beat slow. He had gone through a lot for the first time, but there was much more to come.

"Thanks, Dad," he breathed into my shoulder.

"I'm not your father."

"I know - that's why it's good," he said.

Just before he left he nudged my arm with a closed fist and said, "I'll call you, Sir."


THE END

# RESCUE OF A PUNK

A little later than usual that night, I locked up my leather/sex toy shop and began my usual stroll home in the early evening mist. It was only a few blocks in the mixed industrial-warehouse-residential South of Market neighborhood I prefer. Out of the corner of my eye I caught a glint from the sharp eyes of a motorcycle rider roaring down the street in my direction, but I paid no attention. Especially in that section of San Francisco, a 200 pound 6' 5" guy in leather gets a lot of glances, many of them quite lascivious.

We both stopped for a red light and I glanced once in his direction. I got the impression of a blond punk on a hand-painted blue Norton puffing dark exhaust to add to the air pollution. He wore a black leather jacket - who doesn't these days? - and baggy pants with lace-up boots and no helmet (as usual). Then the light changed and I started across the intersection.

Immediately I realized from the sound that he was trying to beat the oncoming traffic to turn left before the oncoming cars could get under way, which brought him and me into a collision course. Sure enough, he practically ran me down in his illegal turn but he hadn't figured on the railroad tracks, relics of older, simpler days, that looped through the intersection. When his front wheel caught those damp tracks at the wrong angle, down he went, skidding into the curb with a muffled whack of his unprotected head almost directly in front of me.

My first impulse was a sneer - he deserved whatever he got. Then my better nature kicked in and I hurried to him in case he had really been hurt. I prefer to induce my own damage on punk kids.

One wheel of the bike was still spinning in air but the motor had stalled. The kid was flaked out, half off the bike, his head on the sidewalk, but he wasn't bleeding. The baggy pants had camouflaged what appeared to be good solid, muscular legs, and there was a wide gap between his half-shirt and his belt that showed that honey-hued smooth skin that only young blonds can produce. His face was almost triangular with unusually thick, blond brows and cupid lips. His short hair was cut in a half-Mohawk with a hint of blue dye. A long silver bangle dangled from one ear, and the other ear had about six rings.

His eyes were closed, but as I studied him they opened and looked hazily at me with a blue intensity that was startling. Slowly a wan smile developed, although his head must have been pounding from that curb-stone kiss.

"You OK?" I grunted a little sarcastically.

"Am I in heaven?" he asked shakily, searching my dark eyes and scanning my salt-and-pepper beard and hair, perhaps looking for a halo. Nobody ever accused me of anything close to holiness and, after nearly running me down, his question irritated me.

"Not yet," I snarled and started to help him up. He was a solid armful, more muscular than his clothes suggested, but he wavered when trying to stand alone. Shit, I thought, now I've got him on my hands, although the thought didn't bother me too much. I studied him for a moment, then propped him against a light pole and wrestled his bike to the sidewalk. I turned off the ignition and slid his keys into his pocket while his eyes followed my moves blearily. He was in no shape to take care of himself at that point. Without further comment I picked him up, slinging him over my shoulder, and continued my walk home.

He stammered and sputtered and wriggled around on my shoulder, making indignant sounds which I ignored. In that position his ass was alongside my face, and it was a neat, rounded one, rather small but very firm. As we moved down the street I thought I could feel a growing hardness poking my shoulder which his ineffective struggling was doing nothing to diminish.

"Where the fuck we going?" he finally got out, his voice bumping with my strides.

"My place, near the end of the block," I answered without further explanation, and he quieted, apparently thinking. Then he began to jerk in my arms, which I didn't understand at first, but then realized he was giggling, and I could feel that tight, smooth belly spasming close to my face. I knew what he was giggling about; it must have looked pretty funny to a casual onlooker, the tall, bearded daddy-type in leather stalking down the street with a young, blond punk slung over his shoulder. If he was giggling I guessed he wasn't in too bad shape. By the time we reached my door I was also smiling, but more from what I had in mind than from our appearance. That cute, rounded butt was giving me plenty of ideas.

I punched in my code and the door opened automatically. Instead of climbing the stairs to my apartment I turned down the hall and slid him down to his feet in front of a door painted black. He stood there staring up at me, his blue eyes clear now and questioning. He only came up to my shoulder in height.

First I went over his head feeling for bumps and bruises. There was a lump starting, but by parting the short, spiky blond hair I could see that there was no bleeding. He stood quietly while I examined him, and I knew his eyes were on my crotch. He was getting pretty cocky, but at least I knew he was all right. I opened the black hall door and shoved him into the darkness, moving in closely behind him.

I flipped a switch and a soft drum beat started, part of a tape of sex music I frequently used. Then I eased upward on the dimmer switch, bringing in scattered red lights that dimly illuminated the black walls with my toys hung neatly in position. The sling hung invitingly in the center of the room, and he gasped softly when I clicked the door shut.

Without waiting for him to digest the implications, I roughly peeled his jacket off, noticing the good deltoid bulges under my hands. "What are you doing...?" he began, starting to turn toward me, but I whirled him around and pushed him forward, next to the head end of the sling. I quickly raised one of his arms and snapped the manacle hanging from the sling chains around his wrist. "Wait!" he cried once, starting to struggle, but I clamped one long, ham-hock leg around him and soon had the other wrist secured in the other manacle. He knew he had had it.

The shackles were attached low on the chains, since they were placed for keeping a slave in position while lying in the sling. This brought his ass out when he tried to move away, but those fucking baggy pants had to go. I reached around the front and unfastened them, pulling them down to the floor in one swoop. The tight, white briefs were the next to go, and there was that pretty white ass with a distinct tan line apparently made by very skimpy bikinis. I immediately brought my swelling leather crotch tight against those beckoning buns.

"Hey, man, whatcha doing? I'm straight - I got a girl friend that I fuck every chance I get - lemme go!"

My answer was to reach around and pinch his perky nipples as I ground my crotch against those hot spheres of potential joy. "Straight, huh," I grunted, "I'll show you what's straight, and it'll be straight up your shithole, and you'll love it." I twisted both nipples pinched between my fingernails, and he struggled harder, making me the same way. His pecs made nice, solid handfuls.

"Come on, man," he pleaded, "I don't go that route, I'm no fuckin' faggot!"

He was beginning to irritate me again, and I knew the best treatment for that. I brought a leather paddle (my own design) and made sure he saw it before I brought it down hard on one of those bubble buns. "Yeow!" he yelled, and again even louder when I treated the other side to a matching taste. A few more whacks on both sides brought up a healthy pink hue and I was beginning to enjoy it. He tried to move away, but the wrist shackles and his pants around his ankles prevented much movement.

"Repeat after me!" I commanded between slaps. "I will not try to run people down on my motorcycle ever again!"

"OW! - OW! Come on, stop it, man, hey - OW!"

"Repeat after me!" I snarled again, with increasing pressure with the paddle.

He gasped and groaned but eventually began to chant, "I will not run - OW! - people down with - OW! - my motorcycle - "

"Ever again, SIR!" I commanded, placing the swats to even up the color scheme.

"Ever again, SIR!" he finally gasped.

"Repeat after me: in the future I will always wear my helmet!"

"Aw, shit, man - OW! - helmets are for faggots!"

"All the more reason," I snarled, concentrating on the underside of those pretty buns, close to the gate to la-la land. "Say it!"

"I will always wear my helmet - hey stop!"

"Helmet, SIR!" I roared.

"Helmet, SIR!" he repeated, his struggles seeming to taper off. Maybe he was getting numb, or starting to like it too much.

I put the paddle away and decided to get rid of those pants. First I had to unlace his boots which took some time, during which he kept up his protestations about how straight he was and what a bastard I was for putting him through this. I let him rant, but noticed he didn't put up much resistance when I lifted his feet to slip off the boots and pants. Soon he was naked from the waist down but with his flimsy half-shirt still in place. That went with one prolonged yank. He had damn fine legs covered with soft down and a flaming pink butt that looked better all the time. At least he looked and smelled clean. I decided to take a better look.

I spread his feet wide, exposing his ass crack that carried some of that blond fuzz. I stood between his feet and then, stooping, picked him up by his lower legs and moved backward, leaving him suspended between my hands and the manacles on the chains. It was a good view, and his kicking and squirming only improved it.

"Come on, guy, what are ya doing? Let me down, huh?"

I still wanted a closer look at the virgin hole I was planning to plunder, so I bent his knees and moved forward, bringing his spread ass up for my view. There it was, that pink portal that winked at me from the perfect valley between two hills. It was too pretty to ignore, and I bent to lap those clutching, pink lips that only a 19-year old blond can offer.

"Man, what - ah, oh, man, what the fuck - yeah, oh yeah - " he stammered.

He tasted and smelled like "boy" - there is no other description that fits. Youth and young sweat and hot, young flesh all combine to make boy ass a feast for the gods. The usual routine for a lot of guys is, I know, "beat 'em and fuck 'em"; my preference is "beat 'em, eat 'em, and fuck 'em", but maybe I'm just greedy.

I probed my tongue up his bunghole while he squirmed and bucked, this time cooperating. His growls and complaints changed to urging me on. Even when I switched to biting big mouthfuls of tender buns he groaned with appreciation. When I had finally had

106

enough, the teeth marks showed clearly and his ass hole was open and dripping, ready for just about anything.

He was getting heavy. I lifted him high and flipped him, ass over head, onto the sling. The manacles swiveled properly, and after he landed on the leather with a satisfying "Slap" he was automatically in position for the next stage.

The first thing I noticed was his cock, stiff as a fuckin' ramrod, slapping his belly as he fell into position. The size was a surprise, a good eight inches which might have looked ordinary on me but was hefty for a guy a foot shorter. I always found little guys with big cocks a special turnon for some reason.

He had barely recovered from the shock of his landing before I had his ankles shackled in the stirrups of the sling. "Oh, shit, man, what are you goin' to do now - " he groaned, kicking somewhat ineffectually. His cock and asshole were sending him new signals and his resistance had become token. In the meanwhile I had to get out of some clothes now that he was securely stowed. My leather pants were becoming too much like a chastity belt.

He watched me closely as I slowly stripped off my boots and leather pants in his full view, leaving my leather shirt and jacket on. The little punk had really turned me on, and when my prick snapped up free of the pants he gasped and breathed, "Oh, shit." Ten thick inches shouldn't be considered excessive for my height, but it usually gets that reaction. He gulped a few times, realizing, I suppose, how much damage that rod could do. I stroked it a couple of times as I walked back to the head end of the sling.

First I unsnapped the pillow chains, letting it hang down from the sling. Then I lowered the head end of the sling to put his head in the proper position, and pushed down on his forehead. That brought his face at my crotch level, right where I wanted it. He was nearly upside down, looking smack into my sweaty crotch, and his eyes widened as I moved forward.

"Oh, no, man, you're not going to put that in my face - no, no, please - "

"Oh, yeah, kid," I gritted, liking the pretty blond face even more upside down. His lips gaped open, his eyes riveted on the stiff prick and heavy, hairy balls he was going to become very familiar with. I moved closer and he tried to turn away, but I kept his head in place without much trouble. I set my balls on his nose, my cock extending down over his face, and I could feel his hot breath whispering among the hairs.

"Fuckin' punk kid," I snarled, "think you're pretty wild with your Nazi hair-do and your earrings and your black leather, which you know nothing at all about but think it's 'kinky'! Shit, kid, you don't know what kinky is! That fuckin' girl friend of yours will never be able to set your head right. You're goin' to find out what manhood and leather are all about!"

I couldn't see his eyes, although I wanted to. They might be glinting with hatred, wide with fear, or just welcoming the challenge. Who could tell with these punk kids?

I pulled back and tilted his head back even more, positioning the head of my cock at those rosebud lips. His teeth were grimly clamped shut, but pressure of my thumbs on the sides of his cheeks pried his mouth open and I shoved a few inches through those pouting lips. Jesus, it was a hot mouth! His pink lips stretched deliciously around my cock shaft, and I could see the tortuous veins swell even more when his tongue scraped around the head. He took a couple more inches before he gagged and I pulled back temporarily, only to start fucking his face in short strokes of about six inches or so. His head wobbled from side to side, trying to accommodate my fat dick, but he had stopped fighting it for the moment at least.

I had my own struggle going on. The temptation to shoot my wad into that young mouth was enormous, and I had to grit my teeth to save it for an even better occasion. Even then I had to pull out suddenly, feeling my juice beginning to boil. I looked down at him then, and he was staring at me with what I interpreted as fascination rather than animosity. On impulse I bent to kiss that cupid mouth, gathering him into my arms like the little bundle he was. His lips moved under mine, at first hesitantly and then more openly. I nearly lost myself again before I pulled up.

"It takes a man to suck a man," I noted, more gently than I had expected.

That pretty ass still beckoned me, and I moved to the foot of the sling where it was laid out in all its glory. I pulled him down to hang off the leather, and his stiff cock jerked upright as I touched him. His hole was hairless, but silky, blond strands decorated his perfectly matched balls that were tightly clustered at the base of his cock. I bent to tongue them and his cock lurched repeatedly. He was strangely silent.

The one thing that set of gonads needed was a leather cock strap. I snared one from my collection, one with flat studs that would set them off properly, and encircled them roughly. He sure didn't need a cock strap to keep an erection; he was bone hard. His hole had tightened up again. Maybe he was a virgin after all.

I'm really not into rape. So far his reactions had been unconvincing resistance to the ideas rather than the acts themselves. He just needed a little persuasion. Like most punks, he didn't know what he wanted and somebody had to come to the rescue.

I donned a plastic glove, squirted some lube onto one finger, and started circling his hole with my greasy fingertip. His eyes were fixed on mine and there was a trace of hysteria in them. I could almost hear the gears grinding in his head. Still he was silent.

Slowly but steadily I introduced one finger, and he grimaced a little. His cock gave another lurch when I passed the sphincter, and then I was in, probing his tiny taut rosebud, bringing a gasp to his lips and a persistent rise to his prick. I couldn't resist stroking that boner as I moved my fingertip, and he nearly bent double with the double whammy. "Ugggh, Christ!" he groaned, and actually started pushing back, wanting more. Obligingly, I slipped another greased finger in, and his groans grew even louder. A little more massage and a few in-and-outs and I figured he was ready. I sure as hell knew I was.

I couldn't find an oversized condom in my collection, so it took a while to struggle into a normal one. He watched me with increasing uneasiness and started to whimper. "Please, man - don't stick that huge prick in me - I ain't gay - I never been fucked - "

I grinned in anticipation. "Yeah, you got a lot to learn in the leather scene, kid, and your next lesson is coming up, right now. Your cock says you want it, your ass says you want it, and you're going to get it," I finished grimly.

I squirted some lube over my cock and reinserted my fingers, just to check. It was ready. Slowly I substituted my cockhead for my fingers and pushed steadily into his shitchute. God, he was tight! He yelled once and grabbed the chains holding his shackles; his eyes were closed and his teeth clenched. His young heat enveloped me as I pressed on, but it wasn't long before I was in him to the balls. I let it rest for a moment, more to still my impulse to shoot than for his benefit.

His entire body was rigid and that cupid mouth was tense, but as I watched, the tension gradually drained and I felt his ass relax. The cupid lips became pursed and he breathed deeply, his eyes firmly closed. His grip on the chains was casual, more for a feeling of security than assistance, it seemed. The rock music beat hammered subtly, a synthesizer wail alternating with voice-over gibberish. Maybe he understood the words but I didn't. I could only imagine the fantasies coursing through his brain.

Slowly, almost imperceptibly, I began my movements in and out. My balls immediately started to scream for release, and I slowed even more. He had started to stiffen up again as I moved, but I could feel the relaxation spreading from his brain to his mouth to his belly, his ass, and finally his legs. His cock was filling his navel with precum. His eyes were still closed.

I settled for long, slow strokes, pulling most of the way out before a slow slide into his middle. Soon he began to weave his ass a little, wanting to feel my prick moving in his gut. I knew the feeling and gave him a little side-to-side along with the in-and-out. Soon there was a fucking smile on his face, and I knew he was hooked on getting fucked for life.

His happiness wasn't exactly what I had in mind. He needed some punishment, something to shake a few screws into new slots in his brain, so I picked up the pace, hammering harder and harder into that pretty ass, longer and deeper strokes for my own enjoyment. I grabbed his throbbing dick and jerked it a few times, and that brought a more urgent groan and a broader smile to his lips. My balls crushed against his butt with every thrust, and they were unstoppable in their demand for boy-ass now.

I began to jerk him roughly, his cock leaking juice over my hand, and while I impaled him with all ten inches he nearly convulsed and began to spurt streams of boy cum over his belly and chest while I pounded his ass unmercifully. "Oh, Christ, yeah - yeah - yeah - " he screamed, writhing within the confines of his shackles. His eyes were open now, glued to the action between his legs. I couldn't hold back any longer either.

I dropped his still-spurting cock, pulled out, quickly stripped the condom off, and finished off with my hand, shooting great globs of cum over his belly to mix with his. He watched it all, his eyes almost black with the intensity of his experience. His mouth hung open, slack and moist. He twitched as each spurt splattered on his golden skin now flooded with male juice. Then his eyes held mine for a long minute, his expression softening gradually into an intimate kind of peace.

It took me a while to recover, also, but finally I wiped off his belly with a towel and unshackled him. He didn't immediately move away from his shackled position, just relaxing and collecting his thoughts, I guess. When he did start to move I helped him to his feet, and he immediately leaned against me, his face against my chest.

"You OK, mate?" I asked, my throat gravelly.

He silently mouthed the word "Mate", as if it was a new word. Perhaps it was. I had to move away. He was a beautiful young stud but just a punk kid, after all, and he probably hated me now. He dropped his arms and looked at me. I thought he was going to say something, but apparently he changed his mind and looked away. Then he looked back at me. "OK if I keep the cock strap - Sir?" He actually said "Sir".

I grinned. "Sure, I guess so. Why do you want it?"

"It goes with my jacket."


THE END

# DANGER: WRITER AT WORK

I settled myself at the computer-word processor that Sunday morning in the mood to write another short story, perhaps inspired by something that had taken place the night before. As usual I was nude except for my black leather chaps, black cotton jockstrap, and bike club overlay vest. The roughness of leather against my skin and its aroma in my nostrils are as necessary to me as food. Jack, my slave, was tending to his usual Sunday morning chores, that of removing the road grease and splatters from our motorcycles before we set out later for a leisurely run. That cleaning job usually takes an hour or so and five or six toothbrushes, the only tools I allow him to use.

I was still trying out an "ergonomic" chair that someone had talked me into buying. You know what they are? Actually you kneel with your knees spread on a low bench with your ass on a higher bench and your feet extending behind you off the floor. That puts you on a decided tilt but it is supposed to be good for your powers of concentration. To me it seemed too much as if I was praying. So far I was not impressed.

So how do we start?

```
(working title) THE MAKING OF A SLAVE

     Bart first saw him as he gunned his
Harley into the parking space outside his
apartment building.  The kid was locking
his bicycle to the parking stand, but his
dark eyes under the dirty blond short
spikey hair were fixed more on Bart than
on the chain in his hand.
     "Hi," Bart grunted shortly, in a quick
glance taking in the compact body nude
except for his tight Speedos and Adidas.
```

He liked the way the almost fuzzy, light hair curled around his prominent nipples and adorned his trim, muscular legs, but he wasn't about to show his interest as obviously as the kid was doing. That wasn't his style.

"Hello." The voice was soft and rumbling, seeming to leave something unsaid or maybe inviting further response from Bart. When none was forthcoming, Bart merely concentrating on settling the bike on its stand and retrieving a few items from his saddlebag, he continued. Bart had been sure that he would.

"My name's Carl - just moved in. I'm a student at the University."

"Um, hum," Bart responded noncommitally as if he knew that already. He was aware that the boy's eyes were taking in the swelling biceps and pectorals apparent under his black body shirt and the thick, muscular legs under his black leather chaps. Par for the course.

"Mine's Bart," he said shortly, straightening from his tasks. He intentionally allowed his eyes to drift from those arresting dark eyes to his crotch that looked pleasantly packed before starting for the door. He also was not surprised to find Carl just behind him as he reached the elevator. As they waited for the creaky car to arrive, Bart decided he should make a little more effort.

"What's your floor?"

"Six."

"Same as mine," he mentioned casually, and no more was said until they both left the elevator on the sixth floor. Carl hesitated as Bart turned toward his apartment. "Follow me," he ordered shortly without looking at him. Of course the boy obeyed without question.

"All finished, sir," Jack reported, a thin sheen of sweat glistening on his bare chest and legs, above and below the skimpy shorts he was required to wear for the neighbors' benefit.

So far my fictional heroes hadn't done much for me, so I stopped everything to inspect the bikes. Jack would be hurt if I didn't.

"What about that streak there, on the bottom of the exhaust pipe?" I growled, finally spotting something that would warrant a complaint.

"Oh, sorry, sir," Jack mumbled, and immediately fell to with a cleaning cloth. It was not accidental, I knew, that his position brought his firm, round ass up for my review. Other than a not-so-gentle nudge with my toe, I ignored his ploy and thereby saved the neighborhood once more. I returned to my own work.

> Once in the apartment, Bart went to the refrigerator and snagged two beers, tossing one to Carl without comment. They cracked the cans and took a swallow, their eyes meeting openly over the frosty brews for the first time. Still without speaking, Bart put down his beer and stripped off his shirt, noting the appreciative response to the exposed merchandise. Without stopping, he unsnapped his chaps and unzipped the legs, allowing them to fall behind him. The boots came off next, and then the faded levis. Carl gulped his beer hurriedly, watching the entire stripping process in silence. The massive meat swinging from the dark crotch claimed more attention, especially when Bart allowed it to twitch slightly on its way up.

"Ready to go, sir," Jack reported in again.

"Get in uniform and bring me your chain."

OK, now what would they do? Maybe - no, too tame. What about - no, not really in character -

I was still thinking when Jack returned, nude and

collared, chain and shackle in hand. I noticed with satisfaction that he had on my favorite studded leather cockring and ball stretcher. His cock arched thickly from his blond bush - he always became semi-hard when he put that on. Of course I ignored that and shackled his ankle securely to the heavy leg of the work table I had made myself for the computer and printer. Before I went back to work I couldn't resist giving his swinging dick a back-hand cuff; that brought a gasp from his mouth and full rigidity to his cock.

"Come here," Bart ordered gruffly.
"Sir?" Carl stammered.
"That's right," was the response. "Turn around - yeah - those shorts have got to go." Without ceremony Bart stripped off the shorts, exposing the creamy, rounded ass with its light brown fuzz. He swung him around and, as he expected, found himself the target of a sizable, stiff cock pointed directly at him.

"Put those back on me," he pointed to his chaps crumpled stiffly on the floor. Carl looked at them uncertainly but picked them up, not sure what to do next. Bart took them from him and wrapped them around his waist, snapping them in place.

"Zip the legs," he ordered brusquely, holding the flaps together in his crotch. Again Carl looked confused, obviously never having been this close to leather before. "Up here, asshole," Bart snarled, and Carl hurriedly knelt and began to fumble with the zipper. His hands brushed Bart's heavy, hairy balls as he worked, and it took several tries before Bart was again encased in leather. By that time the thick prick was rigid and Carl was trembling more than ever. He rose again and stood stiffly, waiting for orders.

"Lie down."
"Sir?" Carl asked again, his face

flushed, still fascinated by the huge
cock thrusting from Bart's groin.

Bart frowned.  "That's a term of
address, not a fuckin' question," he
growled.  "Like this." Abruptly he put
a leg behind the boy's and effortlessly
flipped him to the floor. He stood over
him, looking down appraisingly. Carl's
mouth gaped open in surprise. Bart was
satisfied with what he saw.  There was
just the right amount of fear and apprehension on his face.

My left foot began to tickle and then I realized that
it was Jack's tongue, lapping the sole and then focusing
on my big toe between pursed lips.  I should have
punished him for interrupting my train of thought, but
I have always been a sucker for foot worship.  I tried to
concentrate on my story as the gentle thrills coursed
through my legs and up my spine.

Bart stepped down with a bare, raunchy
foot on the slavering face of his new
slave, forcing his mouth open and his
tongue to protrude.  Roughly he forced
his big toe into the slobbering mouth,
pleased with the warm, wet clasp of the
thick lips.  The dark eyes looked up at
him helplessly with revulsion mixed with
fear, and Bart could see a shudder
contort his entire body as the reality
of his situation became clearer.

Gradually the withdrawal diminished
and the lips began to serve as intended.
Bart switched feet for a moment until he
was satisfied that his point had been
made.  Then he transferred his moist foot
to the boy's crotch, mashing the rigid
rod roughly against the flat belly.  The
stiffness only increased.

Since I had not objected to his foot service, Jack was
becoming bolder.  Flicking through the coarse black hair
of my calf, he was probing the crease of my bent knee

117

firmly planted on the "ergonomic" bench. My cock was beginning to stretch the jock.

"Damn it, Jack, you know I'm trying to write and all you can think of is your own pleasure! I ought to get out the cat-o'-nine tails."

Jack's face lit up. "Want me to get it?"

"No, no, I've got work to do. Just sit there, or lie there, or whatever you want. I'm starting to get into this now."

> Bart's thick prick matched the boy's in rigidity as he watched him cringe. Carl had initially tried to ward off the foot pressure by grasping the hairy leg, but his grip became a caress as he surrendered more and more.
>
> Bart used his big toe to roll the spongy cockhead across the washboard belly. The hairless balls seemed to rise up in response, and so he gave them a little mashing, too. The boy's body started to curl around the pressure that was

Although Jack had knocked off his foot and leg worship, my cock seemed to persist in its upward course and the jock was becoming uncomfortable. I looked down between my legs and saw the reason. Jack's mouth was enclosing my cotton-sheathed cockhead and his teeth were gently but persuasively nibbling. I guess my position on that fucking "chair" was too much for him to remain subdued.

"Shit, man, how am I supposed to write this story with you swinging on my dick?"

His blue eyes looked up innocently at me and he shook his head without relinquishing his hold on what was now a rearing hardon. It was the old slave trick - entirely innocent, a victim of circumstance where their master's body forced them to do things they would never do otherwise. Hah!

118

just short of pain.  These things can't
be rushed.

Breaking off his gentle torture, he
dropped to his knees, straddling the
handsome face taut with apprehension.
A line of downy fuzz marked his upper
lip.  He probably shaved once a week.
His mouth flew open with the sudden
proximity to all that muscle.

Bart unceremoniously shoved his stiff
prick into that gaping mouth and down his
throat, bringing a choking gurgle from
his victim.  He held it there, deeply
imbedded, until the brown eyes almost
screamed from impending suffocation.

"What's the matter, kid," Bart
snarled, "too much for you?  Your master's got a thick ten inches, and you get
to suck it and swallow it when your
master's in the mood."  To emphasize his
control, he pulled it almost all the way
out and then rammed it all the way in
again, feeling the slave's throat tighten
around the head

I couldn't take too much of that.  Jack was begging
to be disciplined, persisting in sucking in that lips-tongue-
teeth technique that I had taught him - for other times
and other places!  He was stretched out between my legs
and behind me, his cock straight up and throbbing in its
leather harness.  I reached back and, grasping the whole
set in a rough fist, began twisting.  The hot, hard flesh
and studded leather felt good.  The balls were heavy and
full, although they had been drained twice the night
before.  My boy doesn't stay down for long.

It was not until I had twisted a full 180 degrees that
he gasped and relinquished my dick.  Even then there was
a broad smile on his face when I looked down at him, the
crazy bastard.  My dick was stretching the soggy jockstrap
close to its breaking point.

"You need bruisin' bad," I muttered, "but it'll have to
wait until I finish this sequence, damn it!"  I pulled back

further on the seat-bench to remove the temptation and returned to work.

> the way he liked it. Bart held the boy's hands outstretched above his head while he fucked his face. Gradually he watched the fear in his eyes being replaced by desire, and the previous loathing by respect for the man in control.
>
> When the struggling ceased it was time for a new approach. There was more to come, more territory to conquer before the slave could be let off the hook, even for an instant. Cautiously, Bart released the clenched fists but, as he expected, there was no move to resist. He moved forward, his ass a few inches above the boy's face. He watched the dark eyes focus on the brown rosette for a moment and then look up at him with renewed revulsion and horror. At the first sign of an attempt to move away, Bart sat down squarely on his face, funky asshole pressed against the struggling lips.
>
> The boy clawed at Bart's hairy legs, trying to escape the inevitable contact, to fight the demon off, but Bart caught the flailing hands again and chuckled broadly as he fought the boy to acceptance again. He could feel the adolescent fuzz on the boy's upper lip against his asshole, and it felt good.
>
> "Eat it, boy, clean it out, boy, lick your master clean, boy," he almost crooned, smiling as the struggles weakened. He raised himself for a second and heard a quick intake of breath before lowering himself again to the precise spot. He didn't have to wait long before he could feel the gentle lapping of

I could feel a gentle lapping on my asshole. Jack was at it again, this time taking advantage of my moving back on the bench. Taking my cock out of reach brought my asshole into a more exposed position, and he was always quick to take advantage. Jack loved my asshole.

If there is anything I like better than getting my cock sucked it is having my asshole eaten. I groaned, partly because it was distracting me from my writing but more because it felt so fuckin' good. I guess perching on that stupid chair opened me up more than usual, because I could feel his tongue probe into my tight hole almost immediately. I found myself moving back toward him, wanting more and more of that tongue although continuing to stare at the computer screen; that bloody blinking cursor wasn't doing anything by itself.

```
        the velvet tongue.
        "That's right, boy, eat it up.  I got
your face between my hairy legs, and all
you got to do is suck ass until I tell
you to stop.  You like the taste of your
master's asshole, boy?  What's that, you
want to take a breath?  Oh, OK, take a
breath - now back to it, boy, suck ass!"
        Again he cautiously loosened his hold
on the boy's hands and smiled when they
settled on his thick thighs, caressing
the hairy legs that entrapped him.  Again
he raised himself slightly to give the
slave air, and this time spread his ass
cheeks wider before settling back on that
avid face.
        Bart's thick prick rode over the boy's
face, and he pressed it firmly, hotly,
against the downy cheeks and over his
eyes.   Those brown-flecked-with-green
eyes!  They looked up in worship
```

I looked over my shoulder at Jack still busy with my ass. I tried to look angry at his continual interruptions, but the worship in his eyes stopped any complaint I might have made. How do you stop a slave from loving his master, especially when his master loves that loving - oh, you know what I mean.

of the massive hulk bearing him down, bringing him face to face with his true self for the first time in his life. It was time for the next step.

Bart abruptly pulled away and stretched out on top, his weight crushing the boy into the floor. He placed his lips squarely on the boy's, tasting his own musk as he firmly possessed him in his first tender act. The boy melted, his body totally slack except for his lips that avidly partook of his master's largesse.

The kiss was long, tongues smoothing and soothing, fencing and thrusting in mutual lust, although the boy's surrender remained intact. Before it could be disturbed, Bart pulled back again, straddling his torso on his knees. Gently but firmly, he flipped the boy over on his face; there was no resistance. The final phase had begun.

My ass was wet and cool. I had almost become accustomed to having my ass eaten as I wrote, but now it had stopped. I looked around again. Jack was spread out on his face on the floor, his chain still attached to the leg of the table. His cock and balls, stiff and full and swathed in leather, were stretched down between his legs, and his ass beckoned. As I watched he spread his legs wide, and I could see the soft blond hairs encircling his asshole. He looked back at me, his head turned to the side, a shit-eating grin on his face.

The boy lay obediently where Bart placed him. His head was turned to the side but Bart could see no fear in his expression now - perhaps even a hint of a smile. He would have to change that.

The boy's ass bore that soft brown fuzz, and Bart indulged himself for a moment in lapping the firm roundness. As he zeroed in on the beckoning center, he felt an increasing trembling in the boy's limbs.  He knew the moment was at hand.

My cock was still threatening to rupture through the jockstrap and I couldn't concentrate.  Again I looked at Jack, his hunky body spread out, his ass winking temptingly at me.

"Fuck it!"  And then, "I think I will."

The cursor be damned.  If there is one thing I like better than having my cock sucked and my ass eaten, it is fucking ass.  I swung around and straddled Jack, gripping his buns roughly and spreading them.  I spat on my finger and thrust it in, smiling as he grunted with the sudden invasion but knowing he loved it.  He was hot and welcoming, demanding as only a slave can be.

Without bothering to remove the jockstrap, I added more saliva to the rigid mass and replaced my finger with my jock-clad prick.  This time he groaned.  The woven material had to be a little rough on the old bunghole, but he had to be punished for distracting me from my work.  I shoved it in, slowly but steadily, to the hilt, the rear straps of the jackstrap pulling tightly against my ass.

"Oh, man."  That was all he said.  He's a tough fucker.

So am I.  I fucked his ass roughly, there on the floor with the computer cursor blinking accusingly at me.  With each thrust he moaned a little louder, especially when I grabbed his cock and balls and pulled them against my crotch as I plugged him.

It didn't take me long, considering all the preparation he had put me through while I was trying to concentrate on my work.  The jockstrap became even soggier, but my juices were flowing and I could feel his precum oozing into my hand as I twisted and jerked his cock.

When that unavoidable moment came I yelled something and shot hot and wild, his ass coming up to meet me with each thrust.  And at almost the same moment he flooded my hand with his juice, his shouts adding to mine. Our routes took us up and over, his hot ass slurping up my hot juice like a fuckin' sponge. The computer just continued its soft buzz.

> Bart spat on his hand and lubricated his cock. He added more to the tight little hole and then pressed his cockhead steadily against it. As it gradually relaxed he entered the boy, gently at first and then more roughly, his thick prick spreading the boy wide. His leather chaps ground against the firm, fuzzy butt as he fucked him with long, hard strokes.
>
> Other than a soft groan and the continued trembling, the boy seemed totally receptive, acknowledging his master consciously and willingly. With each thrust another step was taken along the road. As he was filled with the massiveness he was relieved of the shackles that had bound him to convention and denial. And when the huge cock spurted its flood, it washed away the vestiges of egocentrism and pretense that had ruled him previously. It wasn't necessary to check for a wet spot on the carpet where his cock had discharged.
>
> That was what Bart had seen in the boy. It would be a long road before he was turned into a man. But it was a start.

"Get ready for our ride, boy. Finally finished the first draft, so we can take off. Another great Sunday afternoon in San Francisco!"

THE END

124

# THAT'S NICE, TOO

"You're not really interested in knowin' all that much about me, are you? I mean, we just met, you're just passin' through town, you fucked my ass good, and we'll probably never see each other again, right?"

He had a point, of course, but I couldn't help being more interested in him than just as a piece of ass. It happened in those golden moments after a hot session when we were basking in that all-too-temporary afterglow of satiated taste buds and drained balls. Maybe it was because he was such a totally masculine young stud who looked like he would be entirely at home on a football field or in a Marine uniform in a landing party. Maybe I was interested just because he was such an excellent cocksucker and knew how to twist his stuffed ass in all directions at once - but I didn't think so.

"Yeah, I really am interested," I said, his blond head resting on my shoulder and my arm around him caressing a firm pec and perky nipple. "I'm a writer - maybe I'll write about you some day."

He jerked his head around to fasten those bright blue lamps on my dark ones. "Yeah?" he demanded. "You mean I might end up in a novel sometime?" I grinned and nodded. Then he sighed. "I probably wouldn't know it anyway - I never read novels." He returned to stroking my spent cock with his fingertips and running his fingers through my dark pubic hair that was beginning to show some gray strands. I repeated my questions about his background, hoping I didn't sound like one of those "What's a nice guy like you doing in a place like this?" types.

He seemed bemused by the idea of telling his story for a while, but then gave this account. I don't know whether it is true or not, but the way he told it, in a matter-of-fact tone, it was entirely believable.

"I'm from Eureka originally. I had two older brothers, but they lit out as soon as they were through high school so I was the only one home that Sunday when my Uncle Ben stopped by with the news. My Ma and Pa were sort of wild, I guess, liked to gamble and I suppose you'd say they were alcoholics - anyway, they had flown to Reno in a private plane to gamble that weekend and the plane crashed. No survivors. The CHP got the word to Uncle Ben, who automatically became my guardian, I guess you'd say. I was only fifteen."

"Hey, I'm sorry - I didn't intend to bring up sad memories - " I stammered.

He shook his head. "That's OK, no big deal now, but I sure cried then, I remember. I kept thinkin', 'I'm a fuckin' orphan', and the tears would roll. I didn't know my Uncle Ben very well. My mother didn't like him and he didn't come around much. He was my father's bachelor brother and lived on a ranch out in the country, but I guess I really clutched onto him in my self-pity. He held me tight in his arms, and I remember how good that felt. My dad had never held me like that, not that I could remember, anyway. He and Ma were always arguin' about one thing or another, and we three kids kept out of their way most of the time. When Uncle Ben told me what had happened I guess I went to pieces and he caught me, holding me close. I remember he had on a brown leather jacket, and the memory of the aroma of that leather is all mixed up with the comfort I felt in his arms."

Unconsciously, I think, he snuggled closer to me, draping one muscular leg over mine and holding my soft cock like a joy stick as he continued. He felt good in my arms.

"Eventually he thought I should try to get some rest, and so he actually carried me into my bedroom and helped me out of my clothes. He was a big fucker - used to wrestle steers in the local rodeos. Anyway, upset as I was, I threw a boner when he undressed me and before I knew it he took it in his mouth and started suckin' me. It felt so fuckin' good I forgot all about becomin' an orphan.

"'You got a beautiful prick, for a kid,' he said, 'Guess it runs in the family.' And then down he went again, shovin' it all the way down his throat and makin' my balls tingle. Before long he also had a finger up my ass and the combination of that hot mouth and his finger up there brought me off in no time. He slurped it down like it was ice cream and I nearly passed out. I guess I went to sleep then, but I remember him takin' off his clothes and crawlin' into bed with me before I nodded off."

"You liked that, eh?" I prodded.

"Fuckin' yeah," he answered. "And the next morning he turned me over and licked my asshole 'till I thought I would burst. 'That's it, just relax, Buddy,' he almost crooned, and he had two fingers up there when he blew me that time and that was even better.

"Anyway, we packed up my clothes and he took me out to his ranch to live. I really liked the ranch, especially the horses, but the old centralized school was for shit. All the students were from ranches or the little jerk-water town and pretty dumb - even Eureka was better than that. And the teachers weren't much better. I never did make a real friend there.

"Uncle Ben had a good sized house that looked like it had never been cleaned. It always smelled like horse and leather. He had a couple of hands who worked there during the day but went home at night. Uncle Ben taught me how to cook, sort of, and I got so I could make supper after comin' home from school on the bus. In the summer I worked with him and the two hands, Hank and Rob, mostly makin' hay and cultivatin' corn. They were both about 25 or 30 years old. Uncle Ben had a pond that we used to swim in after work instead of takin' baths. I remember I felt real grown up when we all stripped down together on the bank of the pond in the evening and dove in, rinsin' off the grime of the day. My only trouble was to keep from gettin' hard when I saw all that bare man flesh.

"Uncle Ben kept a pretty close eye on Hank and Rob, not lettin' them get away with sloughin' off work, but I could see 'em lookin' at me and I was pretty sure what they wanted. I guess I grew quite a lot, workin' hard, and I could notice my muscles gettin' heavier, pretty much like Uncle Ben. He said I stretched up near a foot in two years, and I guess my cock grew a couple inches, too.

"He had a girlfriend, Flora, a widow a few years older, and she used to come around once or twice a week. They'd sit around the kitchen table for a while, swiggin' beers and getting a little drunk, and then they'd go into the bedroom and I could hear a lot of groanin' and moanin' while I was doin' my homework. Then she'd leave and things would be back to normal until her next visit."

"Was there any more sex with your Uncle?" I asked casually.

He grinned and twisted to straddle me, sitting comfortably on my hips and tucking my cock between his buns. "Shit, yeah, all the time!" He began to play with my chest hair (his chest was almost hairless) as he continued.

"We always slept together. At first he just sucked my cock and played with himself, cuming all over his belly, but I started wonderin' what it would be like. Once I dipped my finger in his cum and tasted it, and the next night I started playin' with him and sucked him off, too. He was kind of rough, though - the first time I couldn't get much of his cock in my mouth without gaggin'. He had a real long, thick prick, see, and he got real excited

128

to see me takin' it, and forced it in 'til I just about strangled. I suppose it turned him on that a fifteen year-old kid was suckin' him, you know, a virgin. I could feel him quiverin' all over and he kept thrustin' deeper and deeper until he flooded me with that sweet juice and yelled like a banshee. It was great. Sometimes we even had sex right after his girlfriend had gone home."

Buddy lapsed into silence. I'm sure he was aware that my cock was, by that time, well on the way to stiffness again between his buns that still bore my teeth marks. His own cock was on the way up again, too, but he continued to play with my nipples and my chest hair. "He was hairy, too, like you." I watched the expressions change in his eyes and noticed the curved-lip smile that seemed always just behind the surface. Still there was a trace of sadness there which I couldn't explain. His square chin bore a short blond stubble. I made no comment, and eventually he continued.

"Generally he was pretty nice to me, especially if I cooked somethin' special that he liked, or did some chores without bein' told to. He would pat my shoulder or my ass. I guess he was a little bothered about some things, though - he would frequently say that just because I was keepin' house for him that I shouldn't think of myself as queer or feminine. But I never thought of myself as a housewife or anything like that anyway.

"When we went to bed, though, it was different. Once I started suckin' him he started demandin' it and fuckin' my face pretty rough. 'A man needs to feel he is on top, boy,' he would say, 'but just because I fuck your cocksuck-in' face don't mean I think you're a fuckin' woman!' Then he'd hold me close and I could feel his heart slow to normal after a few minutes, and I knew he liked me.

Then one night he rolled me over and stuck first one and then two fingers up my ass, and then he rammed his big, fat cock all the way in. I remember I cried, it hurt

129

so much, but at least he didn't fuck my face so much after that. And sometimes when my ass was sore I would try to suck him off before he rolled me over. I figured if I could get his cum he would lose interest, and it worked most times."

"Kind of a regular rape," I commented, and he looked at me curiously.

"Hey, don't get maudlin, I didn't. It was excitin' as hell, knowin' I was able to get him so fuckin' hot that he couldn't hold back. He used to slap my ass silly, sometimes, said he liked it pink before he fucked me, and then he'd shove it in and, especially if I wiggled around just right, he would shoot his wad and fill me up with his juice. But after he finished he was real gentle and I slept in his arms most nights."

I couldn't help remembering the scene that had taken place less than an hour ago when I had paddled him, bringing a ruddy blush to those solid spheres while he writhed and moaned happily, rubbing that stiff prick of his against the sheet. "Oh, yeah, beat me, daddy!" he had cried, and I had enthusiastically complied.

"What about this Hank and Rob, did they ever get involved?"

"They turned out to be a couple of real characters. One night Hank walked in after Uncle Ben and I had gone to bed, wantin' his paycheck or somethin', I guess. Anyway, he must have heard the noises from the bedroom, 'cause Uncle Ben was pretty loud, orderin' me around, and especially when he came he would almost scream, but Hank didn't say nothin' at the time. But then I overheard Hank and Rob talkin' one day in the barn. Hank says, 'I know now why ol' Ben don't suck us off no more, Rob. It's that boy pussy he's got now, that nephew who shows off that pretty ass and big cock whenever we go swimmin' in the pond. He don't look queer, but I heard 'em carryin' on in the bedroom the other night, and there's no mistakin' it. Wonder what Flora will think when the word gets out?' And they both snickered. Rob says, 'Wouldn't mind a piece a' that action myself,' and they snickered again and went about their work.

"By this time it was fall and I was back in school, my senior year, so didn't see much of them. Flora still came over but her visits seem to become less frequent. And then one night I heard 'em arguing in the bedroom. Seems like Uncle Ben couldn't get a good raise and she started yellin' about rumors around town that he was fuckin' his nephew and she guessed it must be true and when was he goin' to get rid of that boy pussy so he could give her a decent lay? A few minutes later she slammed out and right away Uncle Ben calls me in the bedroom and fucks the shit out of me, like it's my fault. He sure didn't have no trouble gettin' it hard then, especially after he used a riding crop on my ass and opened me up with the handle."

For the second time that night I regretted not having my toys with me. I was on a short business trip and didn't want to lug all the leather and toys with me. But they would have been fun with Buddy. In the meantime my cock was rigidly riding his ass crack as he unconsciously wriggled against it, his mind on his story. I didn't interrupt.

"During the winter things get tight for ranchers, I guess, and Uncle Ben must have had some financial problems. He started drinkin' every night after dinner, sittin' at the kitchen table staring at nothin', and then he'd yell for me whether I had my homework done or not. He got rougher then, always whippin' me and punishin' me for somethin' and shovin' broom handles and things up my ass. Sometimes he would get so hot doin' that that he would barely get his prick up my ass before he'd shoot. But I knew that after he came he would hold me and everything would be all right. He stopped blowin' me, and I learned to cum by myself on the bed while he was punishin' me. But that's nice, too."

During that matter-of-fact recitation he had lifted his ass and slowly slid down my pulsing pole. His eyes closed and his voice became softer, almost sing-song, and while he didn't move around, his ass caressed and stroked my impaled prick like internal velvet fingers. I gritted my teeth because of the sweetness of that butt and the surging need to fuck him again, but had no thought of interrupting him now.

"I got thinkin', though, of what was goin' to become a' me. Sometimes it was hard to disguise the marks on me, and when I had to shower with the other guys after gym class at school, they would look at me funny because of the bruises. Uncle Ben was gettin' more and more into that beatin' scene, and I was startin' to wonder where it would all lead.

"Then one night - I remember it was the day before my graduation ceremonies - Hank and Rob showed up, demandin' their back pay. Uncle Ben was already pretty drunk and they got into a fight right there in the kitchen. The hands said they hadn't been paid for over a month, and it was probably true, but Uncle Ben claimed he just didn't have any money. I never seen him so mad. Anyway, Hank began whisperin' to Rob and pretty soon they came up with an idea. They would forget the back pay if they could both fuck me. At first Uncle Ben said no, but the more they argued the less objections he put up and then he stomped out of the house, leavin' me with them. I was to be a payment of his debt.

"Hank grabbed me first but I put up a struggle, and it took Rob holdin' my arms while Hank took my legs and they carried me into the bedroom. They tore off my clothes and Hank stripped while Rob sat on me. From the heavy smell of leather and horse sweat I could tell neither of them had taken a bath in days. I was thinkin, if I couldn't get out of this, and certainly Uncle Ben was not goin' to be any help, I had better relax and let 'em have their way and get it over with. So when Hank got my legs up and started to stick it in, I started bein' cooperative, sort of, and at least got 'em to grease me up. Then Hank shoved his stiff prick in and it didn't feel too bad, actually, 'cause I had forced myself to relax."

At that point I was anything but relaxed. Buddy had started to swivel his hips around my cock and was slowly stroking his own ramrod only a foot or so from my face. His eyes were still closed, reliving that night.

"Maybe I was too relaxed. Hank began complainin' that I was too loose, and I didn't dare tell him it was because his cock was smaller than my Uncle's. Rob had stripped down and was playin' with himself, watchin' us, and he had the brilliant idea of both of 'em fuckin' me at the same time. Rob was hung bigger than Hank, but they were both at least average. So Hank flipped around and lay down with me sittin' on top, and then Rob came in from the back. Hank held my wrists while Rob held my ass and gradually shoved his dick in alongside Hank's. My asshole had never stretched that much before, even with the horse whip handle Uncle Ben had used once. Both of 'em began to gasp and groan, feelin' their cocks mashin' and movin' together up my ass. It hurt like shit, but I sort of got used to it after a while. Feelin' both those dongs up there hit spots that never had been hit before, I guess."

Buddy leaned back, his rod swelling to a good nine inches in his hand, and he slowly inserted two fingers in his ass along the underside of my cock. Immediately I experienced at least part of what Hank and Rob must have experienced as his fingers moved along my cock in his swiveling ass. His movements became more purposeful, bouncing up and down in short strokes while his fingers seemed to stroke and clutch my cock in his depths. It was almost like having your cock jerked off inside a hot, clenching ass.

"They really got goin' then, fuckin' me all ways from Sunday, talkin' to each other about how good the other's cock felt against theirs and ignorin' me completely. It was like I was just an incidental factor to them fuckin' each other or somethin', but I was gettin' used to that with Uncle Ben. I stopped listenin' to their chatter and started workin' my ass - "

"Christ, kid, yeah, work it!" I yelled, unable to think of anything but the demands my own cock and balls were making. I'm not sure he heard me; I know I had sirens going off in my head.

"And then I could feel 'em jerkin' and thrustin' inside and I knew they were cumin', and I came, too, all over that fucker's chest - "

And Buddy came, too, all over my chest, his hot splatters spraying me from chin to belly button, tripping my lever and sending me over the top so I spurted my load up his ass and over his fingers. I yelled my joy along with him, and I could swear there were two other urgent, screaming voices in the room with us. In seconds I was drenched with his cum and my sweat, but it seemed to go on and on, tapering off very slowly.

Then Buddy, his eyes still closed but with a happy smile on his face, leaned forward and held me in his arms, the secretions on my chest gluing us together. He seemed to take particular satisfaction in my chest hair that was matted together with his cum. Moments passed as our pulses slowed and our minds began to work again.

"So what happened then?" I asked hoarsely.

Buddy sighed. "Uncle Ben didn't come home that night, and before dawn I shoved some clothes in a bag and left. I never been back."

I sighed also, and then brought his face up for a long, tender kiss. I think it startled him a little, as if he had

never been kissed before, but after a moment he recipro-
cated enthusiastically.  Then he pulled back and smiled
at me.

"That's nice, too," he said.


THE END

Bring up a boy in the way
he should go, and he'll
cum right for you, every time.

# RICKY AND THE MARINES

When Ricky O'Hara Cassidy bent the young, blond stud over the Bush Street bridge balustrade, it was the end of the beginning and the beginning of the end.

When I met him by chance on Market Street a few weeks before that now infamous incident, he looked down in the dumps and I asked why. "I get lonely sometimes, all alone in that big apartment on the hill," he explained. "I haven't had a decent slave since that little Cuban with the big Prince Albert. He was snatched by a big, hairy Bear Master and is now being dragged around town on the back of his Harley."

"With all the available slaves in San Francisco, you ought to be able to make better connections than that," I opined. While no Adonis, his dark good looks and trim body should take him almost anywhere, although I wasn't too sure how good a Master he was.

He shook his head. "I need something special, and I guess I just haven't found it or him yet," and he ambled off down the street, apparently intent on his endless quest.

Ricky had an insatiable appetite for young men, especially those he could train in slavery. To satisfy his craving he spent much of his free time searching likely as well as unlikely spots with a practiced eye for the quick side glance, the stride with a roll on the balls of the feet, the tense hang of broad shoulders that he had come to recognize as hallmarks of the potential stud-slave. He was an expert in spotting them, usually recent arrivals from a small town, or releasees from detention centers, or discharges from the military service when they turned twenty-one. He had the time and the money to indulge himself, and he took his pleasure seriously.

Ricky hung out in train and bus stations, YMCA lobbies, hostel reception centers, and sometimes bars near these spots, eyes peeled for the telltale signs. Sometimes his contacts didn't know themselves that they were gay or that they needed a more mature man to show them the way. Although not yet thirty years old and with no special vocation, Ricky considered himself something of a counselor if not actually a philanthropist as he molded and shaped the expressions of their true natures for those studs bursting with sap for the right Master.

Not all his conquests had been prime quality, he would readily admit. There was the not-too-bright farm boy from rural Utah who had been a real virgin when Ricky spotted him; after relinquishing this unfortunate status in every orifice (with Ricky's assistance), he had written a stupid letter to his family, stating how happy he was in bondage. This was promptly followed by the descent of a whole family of irate religious fanatics, armed and dangerous, around Ricky's head. Then there was the rugged black stud who developed a truly ravenous mouth but eventually reverted to his previous needle habit and almost brought the gendarmes on them in large numbers. But Ricky knew that he had a real find that day when he spotted the muscular blond sauntering somewhat aimlessly from a newly arrived bus in the Seventh Street station.

"Where you heading?" Ricky asked casually as he fell into step with his prey. The blond was several inches taller than Ricky and probably outweighed him by twenty pounds, but that didn't deter him. His sun-bleached blond hair was clipped short but a stubborn lock bobbed over his forehead as he walked. Those big blue eyes with a sparkle for adventure, the way his broad shoulders stretched the faded khaki shirt, the movement of thick thighs and round buns in the marine fatigues, all combined to bring out the satyr in Ricky and pose the naked challenge that was Ricky's prime reason for existence.

The blond looked curiously and almost gratefully at

Ricky, and then smiled tentatively. "Haven't decided," he rumbled, his bass voice resonating through Ricky's ears and straight to his crotch. "I was here once for a few days on leave from the Marines, and I decided to come back for a better look after I got discharged. So here I am."

"Marine, eh?" Ricky tried to conceal his satisfaction. Can I pick 'em or can I pick 'em?

"Used to be. Got my discharge papers right here," the blond indicated a large manila envelope protruding from his knapsack.

Enough small talk, Ricky decided. "Follow me," he said with a wave of his hand, and walked out the door of the station without a backward glance. He heard the clicking of steel heel clips behind him as he led the way to his Porsche convertible in the alley.

"Just throw your gear behind the seat," he ordered crisply. "We'll start with a little tour of the city. By the way, what's your name?"

The Marine was looking at him curiously. His eyes widened when he saw the sporty car, but he did as he was told with his bags. Then, in response to the question, for the first time he looked a little uncomfortable. "Kerwin," he mumbled.

"You said 'Kerwin'?" Ricky questioned disbelievingly, and the blond nodded. Got to change that, Ricky decided. "Mine's Ricky," he said shortly. "Ricky O'Hara Cassidy."

He took a well-worn route to show off the city. Down Market Street to the Ferry building, back through the financial district and China Town, out Broadway to Pacific Heights with its Bay view, and ending up on the top of Twin Peaks which just happened to be near his apartment. He didn't take much time or effort to explain where they were, and "Kerwin" appeared more confused than educated when they finally came to a stop in the garage under Ricky's apartment. At the press of his remote control, the garage door rolled down behind them, leaving them in nearly total darkness.

"Follow me," Ricky said again, leading the way to one of the doors in the far wall. As expected, the Marine, accustomed to following orders, obeyed without question, and immediately found himself in a strange, black room with a leather curtain concealing most of the contents. Bright sunshine flooded the room from one window overlooking the city and bay laid out below.

"View's pretty good from here," Ricky offered, and the Marine promptly strode to the window to look out over the stunning scenery. Ricky did not allow much time for enjoyment - he had other things in mind.

"Grab onto those handles above the window there," he commanded, and the Marine trustingly did as he was told. Ricky pressed a switch in the wall and steel clamps swung out of concealment and enclasped the blond's wrists in broad bands. He was effectively secured to the wall until Ricky decided to release him.

"Hey!" Kerwin yelled, startled and pulling on the unyielding bondage. "What the fuck - ?"

Ricky ignored his protestations and pulled open the leather drapery, revealing his dungeon containing a rack, a sling, a punishment table, and all the whips and toys of the well-stocked torture chamber. Looking over his shoulder, the blond Marine's jaw dropped from the sight of the forbidding array, most of which he could not recognize or understand their uses.

"Let's get those fuckin' clothes off and see what you got, kid," Ricky snarled, unbuttoning the khaki shirt and smiling with satisfaction at the broad, nearly hairless chest.

"What the fuck ya doin', Rick?" Kerwin demanded, still struggling in his shackles but by no means terrorized. Then up came one booted foot, attempting to make contact with Rick as he worked to free the shirt. Ricky stepped aside just enough to avoid the foot, and then

140

quickly snapped cuffs on both ankles to avoid problems from that direction.

"I always wanted a Marine slave, kid, and now I got one," Ricky answered shortly. "Let's see the rest of the merchandise."

With the hands and feet immobilized, there were no problems getting the fatigues down, and the results were even better than Ricky had predicted. The Marine's legs were heavily muscled and covered with soft, light down. His uncut cock appeared about half-way hard and already topping six inches, the moist, pink head peaking out from its hood. And his ass! - man, that was positively mouthwatering. Ricky's prick grew another two inches just looking at it. Twin globes of muscle set off by a tan line apparently made while wearing regulation Marine shorts. Ricky grabbed handfuls of the firm flesh, feeling them quivering slightly but nearly hard as stone.

"From now on your name is Rocky," he pronounced decisively, and the die was cast.

"What do you mean, slave, man?" the newly named Rocky demanded, his nude muscular body rippling in struggling resistance to the bondage.

"Yeah, slave, Rocky. Just start thinking of me as your Master," Ricky growled, his fingers trailing tantalizingly in that beckoning ass crack. The tight rosebud gave a twitch as his finger probed, and Ricky shed his clothes quickly as he surveyed his latest acquisition.

Rocky watched over his shoulder as Ricky bared all. His eyes widened at the sight of the stiff nine-incher bobbing excitedly from Ricky's dark crotch. Ricky was as hairy and dark as Rocky was hairless and blond, but it was Ricky's thick, cut prick that received most of his attention, especially when it grew shiny and slick when smeared with lube from Ricky's store.

But first Ricky had to improve further on the picture before him. From its wall mount, Ricky grabbed a leather paddle with a thick handle. At first he traced the outline of the round moons with the edge of the paddle until he was sure he had the Marine's attention, and then smacked both spheres briskly.

"Uhhh!" Rocky grunted. "What the fuck, man - "

"Not 'man', asshole, Sir to you!" Ricky snapped, giving another, harder slap to first the right one and then the left. A faint pink hue appeared on those virgin buns, growing deeper and hotter as the paddle did its work. Ricky's arm swung rhythmically, each stroke accompanied by a fresh groan from the slave. Rocky squirmed and pulled at his shackles, but every stroke found its mark. By the twelfth one, the ass was bright pink and both pricks were aiming at the ceiling.

"Don't do that, man! Lemme go!" Rocky gasped, pulling hard against the wrist locks.

Ricky dropped the paddle and positioned his overheated cock at the forbidden portal. "Sir!" he commanded, "I'm your Master, you fuckin' dogface!" and shoved his slick prick through the sphincter with one lunge.

"Ahhhhhh!" Rocky yelled, his eyes shut tightly and his muscles rigid from the onslaught. Ricky grabbed his narrow hips and pulled him onto the full length of his cock until his dark, hairy balls pressed hotly against the pink, clenching asshole. Then he stopped for a minute to enjoy the tight heat caressing his rigidity.

Almost immediately he felt the Marine responding, even arching back toward his attacker. Rocky looked over his shoulder.

"Why didn't ya say ya wanted to fuck my ass? Hell, I don't mind. Ya don't have to tie me to the wall! My Sergeant used to fuck it all the time, and he was hung even bigger than you - " Rocky started to rotate his hips around the penetrating prod, his ass channel stroking and sliding in circles, and Ricky's teeth clenched with the agonizing ecstasy. Still he remained still, and it was

Rocky who urged him on. "Come on, Sarge, fuck me!" he finally groaned. "Shove that big tool up my butt!"

This development took Ricky by surprise. He wasn't sure that he liked this willing attitude; he was used to plowing his way into a tight asshole, or forcing jaws open for a satisfying face-fuck, but there was no denying the insistent demand in his balls to ravage that beautiful Marine butt regardless of what the kid said. Starting slowly, he set up a steady rhythm, aided at every thrust by a most cooperative victim.

Ricky reached around front to get a better grip as he fucked, and was shocked at the size of both the throbbing cock and the stallion-sized swinging balls. With cock in one hand and balls in the other, he fucked with long, deep strokes to the steady encouragement of the Marine.

"Yeah, fuck me - yeah, deeper, Sarge - give it to me - yeah, all the way - "

"Shut up, dogface," Ricky gritted. "You're not supposed to be enjoying this! I'm shoving my big prick all the way up your ass and all you can say is 'Fuck me'? Whatever happened to real manhood in the U.S. fuckin' Marine Corps, anyway?"

Rocky didn't seem to care about the image problem; he only seemed to care about the itch high up in his gut, and he tried valiantly, by rotating his hot butt around the long, thick prong, to solve that problem in the best way he knew.

"Yeah, deeper, Sarge, gimme that hot meat - "

It wasn't long before there was no retreat. Ricky was committed almost before he began, and that big hose jerking in his hand was no deterrent. One last deep thrust and he unloaded deep in the spasming gut, and he felt the Marine's cock match his, lurch for lurch. Ricky took a mouthful of Marine skin and muscle, leaving sharp teethmarks in the muscular back until he finally surrendered to the deep satisfaction of conquering his latest slave. Or was it the other way around?

"Jees, Sarge, that was great," Rocky sighed after a moment. "Is it OK if I get loose now?"

"I'm not your fuckin' Sergeant, I'm your Master!" Ricky growled peevishly as he unlocked the restraints. He had to admit, though, that his knees were still shaking from the almost unbearable enjoyment that pretty ass had furnished.

"Uh, yeah, OK," Rocky seemed to agree as he rubbed his wrists where the cuffs had been. "My Sergeant and I used to work out together with the weights and stuff, and usually he'd get real hot and put it to me afterward. He was a real mean fucker," he finished with some ambiguity.

"Yeah, well, so am I," Ricky snarled. "And you can start by licking up that cum you shot all over my fuckin' wall!" Rocky shot him a quizzical glance, but then knelt to lap up the dribbling gobs of his own cum.

Ricky almost envied him that task. It looked rich and potent. "Never ate cum before," Rocky grunted as he lapped, "but it's pretty good, ya know?" Ricky smiled at the prospect of adding to the slave's experience, but that would have to wait a few minutes until he built up another load.

That was the beginning of Rocky's training. The husky Marine took to it like a duck to water, almost too willingly for Ricky's taste. It was abnormal, Ricky thought, to be thanked for chili that the kid was forced to lap up from a dog dish on the floor, especially when Ricky called him "Dogface" alternating with his new name "Rocky". And whenever he facefucked him, Rocky seemed almost as excited as Ricky when he slurped up all that cum straight from the tap. The only thing that Ricky disliked was being called "Sarge", but that seemed to carry with it the slave's absolute willingness to do whatever he was told.

144

As it worked out, Ricky had little use for the cat or any of the other torture equipment as means of punishment since his new slave was so cooperative. Of course he still used them sometimes, but only because he liked to watch the husky, muscular body squirm. The Marine never really complained very convincingly, and that left Ricky uncertain. It wasn't long before Rocky seemed broken to the saddle, as it were.

And so it was that Ricky packed his stud boy and some portable equipment in the car one night and headed for Bush Street. He parked the car in an alley nearby and had Rocky carry the battery-powered equipment to the bridge. Ricky had the kid bend over the balustrade and drop his pants to the street, baring his rock-hard buns to the electrode of the tattoo unit in Ricky's hands. While the usual traffic went by down the one way street, Ricky proceeded to burn his initials, R O C, in bold blue letters into the kid's right bun to establish once and for all his ownership.

From time to time, as Ricky worked, the screech of car brakes pierced the air behind him, the drivers apparently startled by the sight of an ass tattoo going on at that particular spot. No one actually stopped, preferring to believe they hadn't really seen what they thought they had. Rocky had a view of Market Street in the distance and seemed fascinated by the cars and buses emerging from and disappearing into the tunnel below them. Pedestrians on Stockton Street saw only the All-American face of the handsome Marine smiling down from the elevated street, and some gave him friendly waves which he returned with enthusiasm.

But just as Ricky was putting his equipment back in the boxes, a car swerved to the curb and stopped a few feet from the action. Actually it was a Jeep still painted with camouflage colors, and the driver who jumped out was a tall Marine in uniform.

"Kerwin, is that you?" the gruff voice demanded in an authoritarian tone, and Rocky jerked back to look over his shoulder.

"Sergeant Rocco!" he gasped.

"I would have known that ass anywhere after fuckin' it about a hundred and fifty times, I reckon. What the fuck you doin' here, and with your fuckin' pants down?" the Sergeant roared.

"Ricky, here, is puttin' his brand on me, 'cause he sort of owns me now," Rocky explained simply, turning around so that his half-hard cock flopped nearly in Ricky's face kneeling on the sidewalk.

Rocco cast a suspicious eye on Ricky and said, "Oh, yeah?" He snarled down from his six foot-six height at the kneeling Master, obviously not very impressed.

Ricky, from that unfortunate vantage point at the sidewalk level, looked up in near shock at the massively muscular giant towering over him. His rugged face looked as if it had been through a few wars including several broken noses, and the rest of him, all 225 pounds or so of hard muscle, attested to his ability to survive just about anything that might come along. His piercing eyes were almost black as was the short-cropped crew cut. The shoulders looked about a yard wide and the bulge in his crotch looked about a yard long.

The Sergeant's sneering stare was clear evidence that Ricky's position in all this had suddenly become uncertain. Never one to devote much thought before taking action, "Sarge" made his own position clear.

Stooping low, he picked up Ricky effortlessly by his leather jacket collar and his studded belt and unceremoniously deposited him in the rear seat of the jeep. "Get that equipment, Kerwin, and throw it in the back," he commanded. "And pull up your fuckin' pants! I don't like my personal piece of ass on display for all the faggots in San Francisco!"

146

Within minutes they were hurtling down Bush Street in the jeep, Rocky giving directions to Ricky's apartment. Rocky was full of questions and the Sergeant explained briefly.

"After twelve years of Marine shit I decided not to ship over," he growled. "Took my discharge, picked up a surplus Jeep, and set out to find you, since you said you might check out Frisco. Then I find you barin' your all on a fuckin' street! Still the stupid dogface, I see." Ricky, bouncing around wildly with his tattoo equipment in the back seat, was totally ignored until they reached his apartment where he produced his key.

So began Ricky's new existence as number two man in the pecking order. One of the first actions of the new Master of the House was the clumsy modification of the tattoo Ricky had painstakingly placed. Sarge merely added two letters to the brand so that Rocky's ass then spelled R O C C O, but it was understood that Ricky still occupied a somewhat superior position over Rocky at Sergeant Rocco's temperamental pleasure.

Sarge lost no time in clarifying their positions. After they all stripped down, he ordered Ricky to stretch out on the leather-covered mat in his play room. Rocky was placed above him on hands and knees in a sixty-nine position. "Chow down, men, I always make sure my men have a good meal before a major skirmish."

This was a new wrinkle, but neither was really reluctant to follow orders in this case. Ricky, who had previously concealed his desire for the thick, blond prick, sucked it all deep into his throat, no longer constrained by the self-imposed inhibitions of his Master role. Rocky had already shown unbridled affection for Ricky's tool, and delighted in semi-strangling on it for hours on end.

Sarge watched the avid oral action for a while, stroking his enormous cock slowly while relaxing in a leather director's chair. At first he used one hand, but as the action grew heavier, he added another fist above the first. Still a couple of inches of hot meat were visible, the purple head oozing precum to lubricate his hands. He waited until both his slaves were quaking with impending crisis before entering the fray.

"Here ya go, 'Master'", he sneered, straddling Ricky's face. "You been wantin' to swing on this ever since I broke up your little party on Bush Street. Let's see what you can do with it!" He shoved his prick into Ricky's mouth to get it lubricated, and was not surprised when the number two man, with all his enthusiasm, gagged on the enormous length when rammed down his throat.

"I'll have to teach you how to take it like a man," the Sergeant growled, "but I got other plans right now." Pulling it out, wet and dripping, he knelt behind his favorite Marine ass and slowly but steadily he entered his favorite Marine hole.

"Oh, yeah, Sarge," Rocky breathed. "I been needin' that big dong a' yours! Christ, its even bigger than I remember!" Ricky could hear his teeth grinding with the strain, and was glad his cock wasn't in that clenched mouth at the moment.

"Fuckin' aye, jarhead," Sarge concurred. "Best way to keep your ol' Sarge happy is a good fuckin' twice a day!" Unbelievably to Ricky's watchful eye only inches away, that entire rigid shaft disappeared up that Marine butt as if it had been made to order.

As Sarge began to pick up a rhythm and Rocky returned to his cocksucking, Ricky divided his attention between Rocky's cock and balls, Sarge's balls, and Sarge's asshole, which needed frequent lapping from an experienced tongue. The two pairs of Marine balls slapped together happily, moistened by Ricky's slurping tongue. It was a three-man onslaught, an invasive field maneuver under the command of the Top Sarge.

"Lick my ass, way in deep - yeah, get that fuckin'

tongue workin' up there! Now suck on those balls, both of 'em, cocksucker! Yeah! Now suck my boy - take his big prick all the way down! That's Marine dong, man, and it needs a lot of service!"

The demands on Ricky, what with the two sets of heavy Marine balls in his face, the stiff and throbbing cock dragging over his chin, and the aromatic asshole of the Sergeant tempting his taste buds, were tremendous, especially since he instinctively knew that he wasn't allowed to cum until the Sarge shot his wad. Rocky seemed bent on thwarting those efforts, gobbling Ricky's dick in rhythm with the Sarge's cock thrusts deep in his gut. Fortunately the Sarge couldn't hold back for long, and Ricky knew, from the clenching of Sarge's asshole around his probing tongue and the swelling of his balls, when it was safe to let go his own salvo. The Comanche roar from the Sergeant's throat also gave him a clue.

In all the confusion of battle it was difficult to perform all his assignments at the same time, but he managed to catch at least part of Rocky's load while Sarge's whanger was discharging and exploding down Rocky's barrel. His own fusillade cascaded down Rocky's throat amid the shouts and grunts of battle. Any military observer would agree that the three-layer pile of thrusting, groaning virility was a display of massive strength that would make any Marine proud.

The next time I saw Ricky it was again on Market Street, Rocky was at his side, and they looked like they were heading for the bus station. Ricky explained that the Sarge had decided that another slave might be of use around the house, so they were on the prowl. If Ricky's dark Irishness didn't work, perhaps Rocky's blond ruggedness would. Then they turned around and proudly dropped their pants to show me the twin R O C C O tattoos on both asses before setting off down the street.

It was clear from Ricky's happy expression that he wasn't lonely any more.

THE END

# THE 2000 AWAKENING

They arrived two by two. Leaning their motorcycles
on their kickstands in the shadows, their leather clothing
creaking in supple whispers, the men alighted gracefully
and in unison as in most things they did together. The
black bikes, arranged in a line with military precision,
were silent sentinels of the night as the latest arrivals
strode across the narrow alley, their boots grating harshly
on the sandy ground.

To the casual observer the members of each pair might
have appeared somewhat as mirror images. While both
wore black leather jackets, caps, and pants or chaps, the
left side of the leader of the pair bore gleaming metal
hangings - chains, keys, some handcuffs - while the
follower's right side was similarly burdened. In some
cases a steel chain linked them together, extending from
the belt or the black-gloved hand of the leader to a chain
or studded collar encircling the neck of the follower.
Their strides were also matched, the follower one pace
behind and to one side.

Perhaps most strikingly similar were the guarded
expressions on their faces; there were tight lines around
their mouths, shallow furrows in their foreheads, and a
certain blankness in their eyes as if they were distracted
by some outside concern, an element that was personal
and private that filtered their actions.

No words were spoken but the muffled bass thump
of rock music emanating from a low, rambling building
across the alley gave rhythm to their progress. The
sighing of the surf provided gentle background crescendos
that were blotted out by a sudden blast of music as the
Master opened the creaking door of the beach cottage.

The flames of dozens of thick, black candles spluttered
fitfully in the warm breeze admitted through the open

151

door and then returned to their original erection when the door was closed. The air was heavy with the aphrodisiacal aroma of leather and hot wax and male flesh, now motionless as the new arrivals were scanned appreciatively by the earlier pairs of leathermen. A moment later, as if by prearranged signal, twenty arms rose to tilt cold beer into warm mouths dry from anticipation of the unknown. When the new arrivals had opened their own beers and taken their logical place in the circle around the walls of the large, barren room, movements became more spontaneous. The only conversation was an occasional low-voiced whisper. A low charcoal fire in a small stone enclosure glowed red in the center of the room.

Beside each Master knelt his slave, eyes normally fixed on the toe of his Master's boot but sometimes darting furtively toward their companions. They shifted restlessly, uncomfortable in the presence of their Masters in clothing required by their trips. Until their Masters had decided on their next action, they could only kneel and wait.

Then black leather curtains at one corner of the room separated and a giant of a man entered with slave in tow. All heads turned expectantly. This obviously was their host, the initiator of the mysterious invitation each pair had received. His black-bearded face was almost completely concealed in a black leather mask, but the arresting blue flashes glinting from the eye slits revealed his power and authority. His dark visage contrasted sharply with that of his clean-shaven, light blond, almost albino slave who immediately assumed his proper position at his Master's feet. The Master wore only a thick leather harness and a studded leather jockstrap over heavy, hairy muscles; the young slave was devoid of any covering and had been freshly shaven so that not even stubble appeared on his head or groin.

Even the massive appearance of the Master was

insufficient preparation for the thunderous rumbling of his voice as he spoke easily above the music.

"We are Masters and slaves together," he intoned, "and this might be called the dawn of a new day. AIDS has now been conquered, a vaccine has been produced, and it is time to reassert ourselves and our lifestyle - prove to ourselves and others that love between masculine men is not only laudable but perhaps the highest form of love that can exist for mankind."

A low rumble emitted from twenty-two throats around the room. While some were too young to remember the onset of the dread syndrome in the early 1980's, all had survived the epidemic through sacrifices of their natural instincts for sexual expression and, after vaccination, were now officially "immune". It would be difficult to find a more robust, healthier group of men anywhere. For the younger men, a cock had never been tasted free of the rubbery condom that sheathed it. They had never known the unbridled spurting of rich cream that their Masters produced in their deeper recesses. Still the specter of a wasting, painful death following days and nights of shared, uninhibited love-making haunted their actions. Their thoughts remained fixed on their mortality. The continued but diminishing presence of friends in the terminal stages of AIDS, for whom the vaccine had come too late, was a constant reminder of the tragic consequences of sex during those early years before the virus was identified and a preventive found.

"Since the beginning," the masked giant continued, "men have needed to express their aggression and sexual drives, and other men have been privileged to service their Masters as recipients of this life force. For many years this practice has been blunted, numbed by concern for our fellow men and by barriers that reduced our sensitivity and frustrated our appetites."

Again a responsive rumbling rolled through the group,

153

perhaps more strongly from the kneeling slaves than their Masters. How many times had they all longed for direct contact, unhampered by the rules of safe sex, to drink of their Master's juices and be filled with his seminal potion. The Masters nodded understandingly at their slaves, their eyes meeting in rare cognizance of shared frustration.

"Although AIDS has been conquered, we are reluctant to abandon those precautions and practices inculcated in us by the threat of death. It is as if we are afraid of possessing our lovers for fear of losing them, a habit of these last decades of privation. We are still terrified of cum, that potent and primeval elixir of manhood - fearful of intimacy that comes with consuming passion."

The giant Master seemed to swell with indignation, his massive arms folded sternly across his chest. He appeared to grow even taller, the masked countenance almost floating above the assembly like a vengeful god.

His voice had grown softer but no less penetrating. He understood the hesitancy, the residual fear that ruled the men's behaviors. The eyes of his audience were downcast, realizing the truth of his words, even as his voice rose again in exhortation.

"No more barriers! No more antiseptics!" He paused dramatically. "No more! The epidemic is over! We are immune! We must dare to be ourselves, to express ourselves and our most basic natures. It is time to discard the barriers to our freedom and return to that closeness, that intimacy that can only exist between Masters and their slaves!"

This time all in the room shouted in support as the truth was finally grasped. Masters' gloved fists rose in imitation of the giant's double-fisted defiance of the biological threat now conclusively resolved, although they had been reluctant to relinquish the old ways because of lingering fear. Slaves clutched their Masters' leather-clad legs, their mouths watering for the previously forbidden skin and juices of the man most important to them.

Before the tumult had completely subsided, the giant spoke again, his hand raised in salute.

"You Masters are all known to me, and I know you have chosen your slaves well. Rod -" he nodded to the tall Master nearest the door - "Chuck - Mike - Jose - Gordon - Keith - Lim - Don - and on this side, Tony - Bill and Tim. Let me demonstrate how I and my slave will mark this occasion." He strode to the small fire in the center of the room, and the slave followed him on hands and knees. He took a few small packets from his slave's hand. "Into the fire I cast these now useless enemies of love, unwelcome companions of frustrating nights, with the hope that I will never need them again!"

He hurled the small packets onto the glowing coals triumphantly. The foils crackled and curled and the faint nauseous aroma of burning latex emanated from the smoke. Immediately he unsnapped the pouch of his studded jockstrap and his thick, rising cock sprang forth as the group watched. He signalled his slave who immediately impaled himself on the bare prick, hungrily gulping the fragrant skin-shaft. The giant's head tossed back in long-delayed joy and satisfaction from the hot mouth on his bare cock.

Again there were shouts of approval and appreciation from the circle as they watched the dark, bearded giant fuck the pale slave's face with his massive, hairy shaft. But he only continued for a moment - it was too excruciatingly pleasant to continue for long. He pulled his slave up and turned him around, his boy's round, pale buns turned up, and thrust his huge, unshielded prick hard and deep into the grasping darkness. Again he stiffened, his face twisting with almost forgotten pleasure. He pulled the slave savagely against his crotch and thrust again and then again, and then gave a howl of primal triumph as he emptied his heavy balls into the ecstatic slave. No last-

155

minute withdrawal this time - no ejaculation on the floor or in his hand - the healthy sperm was deposited where nature intended, deep in the bowels of his gasping, trembling slave.

The room erupted in lustful action. The Masters all ordered their slaves to strip and practically tore off their clothes when their trembling fingers were not quick enough. They dragged their naked slaves near the smoldering fire and threw the condoms they carried in their pockets onto the remnants of the giant's discards, watching the packets scorch and flare into greasy puddles. They cheered as the noxious smoke filled the room, a symbol of their new freedom from the threat of disease and death.

"Take out my prick, slave, and suck it down," Rod ordered gruffly, shoulder to shoulder with Bill and Jose. The naked Stan hurriedly opened his Master's fly and pulled out the beloved, stiffening tool with some difficulty and gobbled it down, heedless of the precum already dripping from the bulbous head. "Ah," Rod sighed as the hot mouth slurped deliciously against naked skin. He had almost forgotten the thrill of a rasping, fluttering tongue on the tender underside of his thrusting prick, the delicious and tantalizing scraping of teeth over the mushroom head. Stan swallowed the flowing sweetness avidly, knowing it was but a precursor to even more delectable essence of man.

Jose grunted along side. "'Ts been a long time, man," he groaned luxuriously, feeding his slave with long strokes.

"Oh, man, suck -" Bill moaned, his muscles snapping as he held his prick deep in his drooling slave's throat. Bill was younger than most of the men, and had a close cropped beard. His stark white teeth were bared in agonized joy as his slave labored to take all that naked cock into his spasming throat. He could not remember when his Master's cock had reached that huge size before.

Rod snaked an arm around his buddies' shoulders as they stood together near the fire, their slaves delirious with the naked lust and power they held in their liquid grasps. "Like the old days, huh, guys?"

"I don't remember," was Bill's answer, staring down at his unsheathed prick in his slave's mouth. "I was too young when AIDS came around."

Groups were forming around the fire, Masters forming small circles with their slaves busily servicing them. The slaves cocks were equally hard, and when allowed to, they were jerking them furiously as they tasted their Masters' juices, some for the first time. This was no time, the Masters instinctively decided, to withhold gratification from their slaves.

Rod became aware of Jose scrutinizing him closely. His swarthy good looks with the curving black mustache and the almost hairless chest spreading his leather jacket would be a turn-on for most guys. Jose's equally dark slave squatting at his feet made the couple special, Rod thought.

"Rod, I -" Jose began, but they were distracted by the giant and his slave. The mysterious couple weren't finished celebrating yet. The Master was kneeling with his elbow on the floor, and his blond slave was preparing to sit on his fist.

"That's it, boy, up and down a little, let me turn a little," the giant was coaxing softly, smoothing the boy's heaving chest and playing with his nipples with his free hand. The giant's other hand and arm were covered with what was apparently Crisco from a can on the floor, and seemed destined to disappear deep inside the hairless ass. The thick dark cock, recently relieved of at least one load inside that pretty ass, was again throbbing tautly just off the floor.

Rod gently steered his slave's head away from his

157

threatening cock and turned it to watch the fisting. Now that it was safe again, he decided that he would work at home on Stan whose ass was still virgin to a bare fist.

Slowly, gently, the giant's slave pressed lower and lower on the huge fist, his face contorting as he forced more and more of it inside. His Master allowed him to take his own time, but was obviously enjoying to the fullest the naked contact of skin with the fiery sponginess of his slave's channel. The boy's long, slim cock, stabbing upward, dribbled precum over his hairless belly.

There were gently encouraging sounds from the spectators who knew the taking of that huge paw would challenge even the most experienced. Every dick was hard around the circle, their balls up tight and ready for explosion with little notice as the tension mounted.

Rod felt velvet lips on one nipple; it was Jose, apparently following up on the comment that he had not quite made. The bristly mustache scraped roughly against Rod's hairy chest, just the way he liked it. Jose's slave noticed and took the initiative; he scrambled between Jose's legs and began to lick his Master's ass, probably for the first time without some impediment. The hairy nest with its redolent rosebud would be cleaned and polished thoroughly tonight!

There was a collective moan from the circle as the blond slave gave a harsh cry and the hand slipped past the sphincter, deep inside. "Oh, yeah, boy," the giant whispered, "yeah, got ya now - way up inside you, kid." Slowly he rotated his arm, and the boy's head sagged forward and then snapped back to loll loosely in total surrender. Rod couldn't take much more of this.

"Get up here, Stan," he ordered. He positioned his slave with ass high and, deliberately reaching into the now common can of Crisco, smeared grease on his hefty prick. "Your first fuck without a condom, Stan," he said softly, and eased it inside the hot, clasping tunnel effortlessly. "Oh, yes," Stan breathed, twisting gently, rotating his ass in small circles for maximal contact with the hot, bare cock.

Stan had never felt a cock without its latex sheath. There had always been a transient drag on the skin, even when properly lubricated. This time the huge prick slid in effortlessly, skin against skin, heated cock into heated rectum, filling him with a warm and throbbing fullness he had never known before. He imagined that he could even feel the circumcision scar.

The familiar sounds of leather on skin distracted Rod for the moment to the other side of the fire, where Tony was lashing his kneeling slave with a cat while the boy sucked his cock, burying his face in his Master's pubic hair. Chuck had bent his slave over his thick, muscled bare legs and was spanking him thoroughly with a gloved hand. But from the expressions on their faces it was clear that this was only a prelude to a more genital celebration. It was only a moment before Chuck released his boy and quickly shoved his bare cock into his glowing butt. Apparently it was none too soon; almost immediately an expression of anguished joy suffused his face.

Gordon's ebony face shone with sweat as he thrust and twisted his naked fist in the butt of his slave who was on his back near the fire. The black Master had his slave's cock in his mouth, timing his arm action with his mouth movements.

Rod had set up a steady, deep motion, thoroughly enjoying his first unprotected fucking in years but in no hurry to climax. Gripping Stan tightly around the hips, he forced his entire naked prod into that hot ass as if it were his first fuck. Bill watched for a moment and then pulled his slave, Joe, next to Stan. Quickly he became nakedly, deeply imbedded in that special ass, and he and Rod smiled broadly at each other, their eyes holding. Jose, still tonguing the nipple, straddled Rod's leather-clad

159

leg and spread his ass cheeks for the full treatment by his slave. Jose's cock rode stiffly against Rod's leg as the Latino writhed against his slave's face.

The masked giant had slowly brought his blond slave into a crouched position, his hand completely inside. As the *coup de grace* he inserted his thick prick alongside his arm and clasped himself in the deep heat of the ass. Involuntarily Rod picked up his pace; he had almost forgotten how good that felt, hand-stroking his cock inside a hot ass, and now his juices were rising in a nearly uncontrollable crescendo. Almost unconsciously he gripped Jose's rigid rod and swollen balls in a rough fist, a Master's set for sure. Stan was shoving back hard against his plunging prick and he knew he couldn't last very long.

Suddenly Bill grasped him around the shoulders and pressed his lips against Rod's. Yes, deep kissing was OK again! Rod responded with his tongue thrust deep into the young Master's throat, the dark beard scraping his face luxuriously. He did not notice that Joe and Stan, soaring high with their Masters' cocks plunging deeply, were also locked in a deep kiss to match their Masters, sharing their own moment of intimacy.

Rod's fingers became engulfed in a warm mouth, along with the thick cock in his grasp. Jose's slave did not want to miss that fresh cum that was obviously boiling near the surface. Rod encircled the rigid prick and ball sac with finger and thumb, thrilling to the additional contact with the hot, wet mouth that sought that special cocktail. Jose stiffened with impending crisis, and bit down hard on Rod's erect tit.

Maybe it was Bill's kiss, maybe it was the jerking and spurting of Jose's cock in his hand, maybe it was the bellow of the giant squirting his second load into the blond ass, the sudden pain in his nipple, or the groans of at least six other Masters in the throes of climax.

Whatever it was, Rod could resist no longer and filled Stan with boiling cum in spurt after spurt, the first unrestrained load the young slave had ever experienced. At the same time he knew that Bill was following his lead, gasping for air as he shot, not wishing to break the kiss between Masters.

Finally they came up for air, their cocks softening for the moment and with huge grins on their faces. They stepped back from the fire which was slowly fading. The floor was slippery with slave cum. Stan nuzzled and lapped Rod's boots in deep gratitude, and the Master smiled down at the slave happily.

The sound of the surf rolling up onto the beach caught Rod's attention during a lull in the music. "The beach! Come on!" he urged, stripping off his leathers and leaving them in a heap before he raced toward the water. At first startled, others followed until there was a mass pell-mell rush down the beach. Naked, they all splashed into the sea, the salt water stinging and lashing the laughing faces and tender assholes. They clasped each other chest to chest, laughing in each other's faces from which the rigid lines of caution and reticence had finally disappeared, happy to be alive again, having natural sex again, happy to be men who loved men.

Everyone, Masters and slaves alike, grasped for bare cocks and stuffed them into their mouths. Assholes that had been barren for years were reawakened by warm tongues and cocks throbbing nakedly in unbridled, unrestrained passion.

And the waves washed away the vestiges of reluctance, the restraint between Master and slave based on the biology of a foreign virus, the fears of contact that had ruled their lives for years on end. They washed away all traces of the scourge that had threatened civilization and had now been banished. When the men finally left those cleansing waves, they were free of the stain of forced abstinence and antiseptic denial. Masters were again free to demand, and slaves would not hesitate to obey.

When at last they returned to the cottage the fire had almost gone out. Their clothes were in piles as they had left them. But there was no sign of their giant, masked host or his pale slave.

THE END

# OTHER TITLES AVAILABLE
## DIRECTLY FROM GLB PUBLISHERS

### GAY/LESBIAN FICTION/POETRY

*The Bunny Book*          Novel by
**John D'Hondt**. The bunny mystique and
AIDS in a feminist setting.
288 pages      Paperback          $11.95        _____

*A Breviary Of Torment*          Poems by
**Thomas Cashet**. Expressions of our love-
hate relationship with torture.
128 pages      Paperback          $13.95        _____
               Clothbound         $28.95        _____

*The Devil In Men's Dreams*          Short
stories by **Tom Scott**.   Gay men's
tales—but the devil made me do it.
246 pages      Paperback          $11.95        _____

*Good Night, Paul*          Poems by
**Robert Peters**. Poems to a lover—"rapt,
comic, wry, and ebullient" for all lovers.
96 pages      Paperback          $ 8.95        _____

*Snapshots For A Serial Killer: A Fiction
and a Play*, by **Robert Peters**. "A startling
and graphic monologue about violence..."
125 pages      Paperback          $10.95        _____

                    SUB-TOTAL        _____

Add $2.00 per book for shipping:        _____

                TOTAL THIS PAGE        _____
          (Turn the page for MORE new titles)

Check or money order to:
                        **GLB** Publishers
PO Box 78212            San Francisco, CA 94107